MUSCLEBOUND
MARIO

Also by Kevin L. Donihe:

MUSCLEBOUND MARIO

Kevin L. Donihe

Eraserhead Press
Portland, OR

ERASERHEAD PRESS
205 NE BRYANT STREET
PORTLAND, OR 97211

WWW.ERASERHEADPRESS.COM

ISBN: 978-1-62105-154-1
1-62105-154-4

Printed in the USA.

DEDICATIONS:

To Ashli Carte: For talking me through the manuscript and getting me unstuck. This book owes its life to you.

To Michael Lee Smith: For giving great advice outside the realm of books.

To Vince Kramer: For playing with toys.

To Erin "Czarina" (née White) Fairbanks: Now you owe me a fancy tie.

PART ONE:
MARCUS

Musclebound Mario stood stoically in front of the green hill that began World 1-1 of the first *Super Mario Bros.* game. No longer was the action side-scroll or the view two-dimensional. It was an immersive 3-D world, though computerized bleeps disguised as music provided its soundtrack.

He took in the familiar yet unexpected scene. His almost supernaturally swollen muscles bulged beneath bright red overalls, his clenched fists larger than human heads.

This was bliss; this was perfection. It didn't matter how he had achieved it. What mattered was that he was here, and that he wasn't saddled with the squat, spindly body of the actual Mario.

He was beyond Mario.

He was the epitome.

He was the second coming.

He was a new creation, beyond fact or fiction.

He breathed in so much air that his lungs would have exploded were he not such a powerful and majestic thing. When he exhaled, his breath exited as a gale and toppled a Goomba that was sliding his way.

His first kill had made him feel jacked-up, like a rabbit in heat. He bet he could fuck like a rabbit, too. His penis was rock-hard. The Mario of lore wasn't a sexual being, but that didn't mean Musclebound Mario had to share his every attribute.

He looked up and noticed a timer, floating above him and to his right. This level was one he could beat with eyes closed and hands tied, but he'd already wasted too much time. He ran past a bush and a smaller hill, hit the first question mark, collected 200 coins and hit the next question mark. A mushroom slid out, and Musclebound Mario absorbed it into his body.

With feet encased in size 60 boots, he smashed his first Koopa Troopa in the Mushroom Kingdom, relishing the fart-like noise as it flattened before fading away.

* * *

Marcus Lovejoy pulled red underwear up over wide, muscular hips. They'd been regular bikini briefs before he had twenty iron-on decals custom-created. All featured the head of Mario. With trembling hands, he had applied the decals to the front of each pair himself.

He slid a tank top down his barrel-like chest, covering a tattoo—a smiling Mario-head that stretched from nipple to nipple. On the shirt, the same character squashed a Goomba with apparent glee as the Princess floated in a thought-bubble overhead.

Before putting on his pants, he took a few moments to flex and pose, watching Mario's head bulge, both on his chest and crotch. He smiled. It was as though his body was Mario's temple. Never would it be truly worthy, but never would he stop trying to make it so. One day, he'd be greater than Atlas. His muscles simply had to keep growing. They had to wrap around the world and become the world. He imagined villagers living atop his biceps, triceps and quadriceps. They would be happy there. No more sadness. No more hunger. He would supply everything they needed and be a kind and beneficent god to them.

Marcus shook his head, came back to himself and

reached for his pants. They were tight yet stretchy, good for showing off well-developed glutes and thighs, but he resented them somewhat for their lack of Mario-ness.

Almost everything he owned was Mario-related, or had been converted to appear as such. He only drank from Mario emblazoned mugs, ate from Mario emblazoned plates. His toilet seat lifted to reveal a Mario head, and, framed atop his TV, was an autographed photo of the inventor of the game, Shigeru Miyamoto.

There were no other photographs in the apartment.

Every day, he attempted to add a new piece of memorabilia to his collection. Money wasn't an issue. A rich relative he'd never met had died and left him half her substantial estate. Prior to that, he'd been a poor kid—his parents barely able to afford the NES console and the game—and an even poorer adult. It felt good to have all the nice Mario things now, to revel in them, to clutch them to his bosom and never let them go. For this blessing, he thanked the Great Mario in the Sky.

Feeling almost ready, Marcus ran his fingers through his blonde, buzz-cut hair and studied his look in the mirror.

It was perfect for tonight's Mario Party—his second to date. It was to be hosted by two local guys he sort of knew because they too were rabid fans. Years before, they had moved into the same house, so they could discuss the game whenever possible and share secrets.

Marcus' first party had been a low-key affair, just a handful of people hanging out at the house. Few attendees spoke with him, and he'd had an argument with one, but he figured that was because he was the new guy. Things would be different this time. Tonight's party, after all, was to be a three-day-long affair, an international gathering of such magnitude that it was held only once every three years.

Marcus felt lightheaded and a little giddy as he imagined being around so many likeminded people. Real world connections would inundate him and carry over into his life long after the celebration wrapped. He needed that to happen. More than anything.

Out of the bedroom, Marcus decided he had time for a quick bowl of cereal. He could pound supplements later. Pounding supplements was important, but not so important as to make him late.

He went to the kitchen cabinet and removed a box of what he visualized as *Mario Crunch*. It was really *Lucky Charms*, but Marcus had gotten quite good at imagining the puffs were Mario Heads and the marshmallows were combinations of Princesses and Luigis. They tasted great going down, and he imagined all the faces mingling in his stomach, growing arms and legs and dancing inside him.

From the kitchen, he brought a sugar cookie to the picture of Shigeru Miyamoto and bowed before it. Though the picture never responded, it felt good to talk to something that seemed to listen.

"Hey, Mr. Miyamoto," he said, lighting two sticks of incense that had been placed in front of the picture. "It's me again."

Mr. Miyamoto smiled warmly, as always.

"I've got a big day ahead of me, and I'm so nervous. But I don't want to seem that way." He placed the cookie below the smoking sticks. "Could you, you know, wish me luck?"

Outwardly, Mr. Miyamoto remained inscrutable. Still, Marcus knew he had done just that.

He bowed again. "Thank you, Mr. Miyamoto. Maybe we can talk longer tomorrow."

And then he was on his way.

* * *

Regular old Mario could never have bounded over four Piranha Plants at a time or jumped over whole staircases without touching a single step; it wasn't in his program. But Musclebound Mario was no 8-bit thing of fiction.

He reached the end of the level and found himself face-to-face with the largest and most imposing staircase yet. Undeterred, Musclebound Mario took to the air. Higher and higher he soared, topping the staircase before going higher still. If he'd been in the game, he was sure his character would have crashed through the top of the TV and into the real world.

The flagpole was just below him. After completing a mid-air somersault, he landed upon it and pulled down the flag with his bulk. Victory music played as he strolled to the castle. Points were tallied. A new flag was raised. Immediately thereafter, his vision went black for a second, and he found himself traveling through a pipe to World 1-2.

The game music changed, becoming faster paced, dark and creepy. It did not intimidate him. He banged his head against a suspended question mark that he knew contained a Fire Flower. He could have gotten one in World 1-1, but wasn't thinking about it at the time. Then, the acts of jumping and smashing had been enough to sustain him.

Now, he needed more.

He pounced atop the Fire Flower. His body rippled with the full spectrum of color before it settled on red. He stood stolidly during and after the transformation, glowering down at a line of Goombas that wandered the floor. In a few moments, the nearest one would be within firing range.

Musclebound Mario prepared himself. His gut warmed, then became blazing hot—but it was good heat. The fire solidified inside him, becoming a spherical mass before rising up and shooting at light-speed not from his hand, but from his mouth.

There was no pain, only intense pleasure as he watched the first Goomba lose its head and limbs, fly up and then fall not to, but through the floor. The second died as amusingly as the first, followed quickly by the third.

Jumping from the question mark, Musclebound Mario blasted Koopa Troopas from their shells and Piranha Plants from their tall, green pots. After smashing a barrier instead of sliding under it, as would the old Mario, he shot fireballs at the floor, ceiling and walls. He wasn't hitting anything that lived, but that didn't matter.

He was shooting fireballs out of his fucking mouth.

* * *

Almost thirty minutes later, Marcus had made it to the house—an imposing Victorian-era structure. The porch was iron-railed; the uppermost window was stained glass. A steeply pitched roof brimmed with decorative spear-topped turrets. The yard was huge, which was good. There were so many cars that he had to park alongside a host of others on the grass.

He exited the vehicle quickly; glad to be free from it. Driving was too chaotic, too unpredictable. Though 28, he still felt too young to get behind the wheel of a car.

Marcus paused outside the door of the house, took a deep breath and reached out. The knob felt electric as he gripped it.

Was he ready for this?

He had to be ready. No choice.

With a twist of the knob, the door swung open. He stepped inside and stood frozen for a minute, not knowing what to say, or if he were capable of saying anything. He'd never seen anything like this. It seemed too big to process.

Marios, Warios, Luigis, Princesses, Piranha Plants, Hammer Brothers, Buzzy Beatles and more packed the place. He felt a little guilty for not having arrived in costume, but that would have obscured his body, his living testament.

A glowing plastic Mario head dominated the center of the room. So large, the tip of the hat was flush against the ceiling. Standing at the doorway, Marcus felt heat radiate from the effigy. It pulsed slightly, as if breathing, but that had to be his imagination. He just wanted it to be a living thing.

"Oh look, it's *him*," Marcus heard someone say. Turning, he saw the man he'd argued with at the first party, dressed as a Goomba. No matter. He wouldn't let him interfere with the good vibes produced by his long-lost brothers and sisters.

Wandering amongst the crowd, he stopped every few feet to compliment someone's look.

"Oh my god!" he said to a man in a Bullet Bill costume that made it appear as though he was suspended mid-air. "That's so fucking awesome! How do you do that? Is it an optical illusion?"

The man smiled thinly and turned back to the conversation from which he'd been pulled.

Spinning, Marcus saw a Firebar like the ones that rotated about the floors and ceilings of dungeons. Each individual ball had a tiny fan concealed beneath, making jagged plastic ribbons move like real fire. He gawked for a while before realizing this was not a prop, but another man in costume.

Marcus ran over to him. "That's so crazy!" he said. "Can I touch it?"

All-but-hidden eyes narrowed. "Can you touch it?"

"Yeah, yeah! I'd love to do that!"

"No, you cannot touch it! No one touches my flames but me!"

"Just the tip of one. Please."

"No! Not any of it!"

Marcus slid away. That hadn't gone over well, but there were so many people and so many chances at forging multiple life-long connections. He just had to keep moving, keep talking.

He crossed the living room into a kitchen where more partiers hung out. His gaze fell on a pretty brunette who wore a horny, red prosthesis that made her back look like that of a Spiney. He approached her.

"Hey, that's great! I love those characters!"

"Really?" she said, sounding Australian.

"Yeah, they're so cute…but deadly."

Her face lit up. "I feel the exact same way about them! And thank you so—" She glanced downward and gaped.

Marcus was confused until he too looked down and noticed his boner, made more obvious by his stretchy pants.

Quickly, he covered the protrusion with both hands. "Oh god! I'm sorry! It's not you! I swear it isn't! I mean, I think you look great and all, but I don't want to— I mean… It's this place, you know. The party. It's so—"

She refused to let him finish. Turning away from him, she stalked off and didn't look back.

A hand fell on Marcus' shoulder. It took a few seconds, but he recognized the hand's owner as Ronnie, one of the two hosts. He wore only a red cap and bushy moustache as costume, but Marcus still thought it was a cool look.

"Hey," said Ronnie. "What's your name again?"

"Marcus," he said, boner diminishing rapidly. "Marcus Lovejoy. Don't you remember?"

"Oh yeah, Marcus." He lifted his hand. "So, are you enjoying the party?"

He bounced up and down a bit. "Yeah, it's awesome! I love it!"

"That's good to hear. Real good." He leaned in closer to all but whisper in Marcus' ear. "But, you know, be cool."

He stopped bouncing. "What do you mean?"

"Let's just say there's already been a complaint or two."

"Against me?"

"People are saying you're a little too…friendly."

"It's good to be friendly," he countered.

"Not always."

Suddenly, Marcus wanted to flail. "But I can't help it! The costumes—they're so great and everyone's so great and I—"

Ronnie shushed him. "I've got the point, and I agree with it. Some of these people spend years perfecting their costumes, but you can admire them from afar, you know. You don't have to bother people or invade their personal space. You understand that, right?"

"Just listen. I—"

You understand that," he repeated. It no longer sounded like a question.

Marcus nodded.

"Good. Think back to what happened last time. Tim got mad, and it almost came to blows. That's unacceptable here. This is a place of Mario, ergo, a place of love. Try to remember that."

"I already know, believe me!"

Ronnie stepped back. "So, you promise to be cool from now on?"

Marcus tapped his feet nervously. He wanted this conversation to be over. "Sure. Of course."

"Really?"

"Yes!" He shook his head rapidly. "Really and truly!"

The man sighed. "Okay, Marcus." He gestured toward a table across from him. "Have some punch and hors d'oeuvres."

"I will." Marcus slapped the man's back. "Thanks, man."

Ronnie winced. "No problem," he said.

* * *

After bounding through a world of trees and defeating a toothless Bowser in an easy dungeon, Musclebound Mario found himself in a water level, his plumber's outfit transformed into a sparkling blue Speedo.

Though it hurt him to say any level was his favorite,

that he didn't love them all equally, he truly savored the water worlds. Eyes rolling back in ecstasy, he took some time to swim around in body-temperature water and enjoy himself.

When a squid-like Blooper began inching up toward him from behind a pink column of coral, he shot a fireball at it. His laugh exited in bubbles as the Blooper's lifeless form flipped over, scrunched up, and sank to its death.

Moments later, a Cheep Cheep advanced on him. Musclebound Mario prepared another ball. Rather than spit it out, he extinguished it in his stomach.

He'd had a thought.

The old Mario could only kill aquatic creatures with fireballs, but what if Musclebound Mario was more flexible in his modes of dispatch?

He lunged at the Cheep Cheep and struck it full in the face with his fist. When he didn't shrink upon coming in contact with the fish, he kept punching. It felt good—cathartic, even—so he punched harder, screaming, cursing, until the fish was swollen and black and blue.

Other Cheep Cheeps and Bloopers stared on in terror. Finally, the victim turned upside down and died.

"You want some of this, too?" he shouted at the onlookers, his voice so powerful others could hear it while submerged.

They clouded the water with their fear-piss before scurrying out of his way.

"That's what I thought, you bitches!"

Musclebound Mario extended his middle finger and turned his back on them all. His path to the end of the level was free and clear so, upon glancing up at the timer, he did a few back flips before dogpaddling out the pipe to continued glory.

* * *

Marcus filled his face full of cheese and crackers at a snack table. He didn't feel quite so jittery when his hands and mouth were occupied.

He hadn't expected to be chastised by the host. He thought they'd hit it off great at the first gathering. But even that wasn't as bad as popping the boner in front of the girl.

Relax. Calm down. Stop eating and go back to the party.

Marcus took a few deep breaths and did just that.

He mulled around, considered approaching two men who were dressed as Princesses, but stopped when he heard their conversation:

"Do you think it's possible that Mario and Luigi had a sexual relationship?"

Marcus shivered.

Near the huge Mario head, he spotted a group of four who seemed friendly enough. All of the men were in costume. The first was a Blooper, the second a Hammer Brother—with another Hammer Brother as a dummy, connected to his side. The third was a 1-Up Mushroom. The fourth appeared to be a flower with a fat green body and bright red petals that fanned out from his head. Marcus wasn't sure what that was supposed to represent.

He paused. Listened. It seemed they were discussing Mario trivia. As that was his strong point, Marcus decided to integrate himself into the conversation.

"Did you know that when Mario was first introduced in *Donkey Kong*, he wasn't—" began the 1-Up Mushroom.

Marcus bumped the speaker as he edged himself into the circle. "Yeah, yeah!" he cried. "He wasn't called Mario at all! He was called Jumpman!"

The 1-Up Mushroom frowned, but continued. "And he wasn't a plumber, either. He was—"

"A carpenter!"

The Blooper scowled at Marcus. "We're trying to have a conversation amongst ourselves."

"But I'm just sharing my knowledge with you."

"I appreciate that," the Blooper continued. "But you should introduce yourself first."

"You're too polite," said the flower-thing. "I'd tell him to fuck off."

Marcus felt blood rush to his face. "What's your problem? And what are you dressed as, anyway? Some stupid flower?"

The man looked askance at him. "You come to a Mario Party and ask that question?" He ran his hands down the sides of his costume with seeming pride. "I'm quite clearly a Panser."

"A *pantser*?"

"No, a Panser, man. You know, from *Super Mario Bros. 2*."

"Oh, now I remember. Lame character." Marcus snorted. "Haven't played that game in years."

The room's atmosphere changed abruptly. People who'd been having their own conversations nearby went silent.

"Say what?" said the Panser.

"I don't play any of the games that came after the first *Super Mario Bros.*," replied Marcus.

"Explain yourself," said the 1-Up Mushroom.

"Isn't it obvious?"

"No, it isn't."

"*Super Mario Bros.* progressed naturally from *Mario Bros.*, which progressed naturally from *Donkey Kong*." Marcus flung up his hands, almost shouted, "Then the second game screwed it all up!"

The Hammer Brother called him out. "What do you mean, *screwed it all up*?"

"Apart from some characters, the second game doesn't have anything to do with the first one! It's all based on some other game that was only sold in Japan!"

"*Yume Kojo: Doki Doki Panic*," said the 1-Up Mushroom.

Marcus waved him off. "Yeah, whatever. The point is

that purity was lost after 1985, and I want no part of the later games. They're dead to me."

"I have the opposite opinion," said the flower-thing. "I think the first game is inferior because it's too easy."

Marcus felt rage build up inside, but contained it.

"And you can't be a raccoon in the first *Super Mario Bros.*," added the Hammer Brother.

Marcus was defiant. "I don't need to be a raccoon."

"But—"

Marcus stopped him. "You kill things by throwing vegetables at them! Come on! And the screen should never *ever* pan up! It should only go from side-to-side!"

"Do you hear yourself?" said the 1-Up Mushroom.

"Don't you understand *progress*?" added the Blooper.

"Not if it changes something that's already perfect!"

The Hammer Brother chimed in. "Wait, I can almost understand what he's saying. The second game *was* a big departure from the first. But, at the very least, you can appreciate the third game, right?"

Marcus shook his head.

"Not even the third game?"

"Not even the third game."

"But it's one of the greatest video games of all time! So rich! So complex!"

"Too complex, if you ask me."

"Well, maybe he wasn't asking you," said a voice from behind.

Marcus turned and saw Tim, the man he'd once argued with, standing behind him. Marcus hated looking at his ugly, pug-nosed face and dark, beady eyes. Not even his Goomba costume could make him look cool.

"Is this guy pulling that shit again?" Tim said to the others.

"It's not shit! It's the truth!"

"Fucking blasphemy is more like it," said the Panser.

Tim poked Marcus in the chest. "You flat-out don't deserve to be here. You care about developing that meathead body of yours more than the games."

"That's not true! This body is a—"

"You cannot have divergent interests and be a true *Marionite*!"

"Wrong! Whatever I do, I do for Mario!"

"You do it for yourself, and that disgusts me. I should have knocked you out cold the first time I saw you. Maybe then you wouldn't have come back!" He turned from Marcus. "Listen up, everyone!" he shouted. "This man is a stranger in our midst!"

Marcus tried to shush him, but he continued to shout.

"He freely admits to hating *Super Mario Bros.* 2 and 3!"

The room went completely silent. Even non-English speaking guests seemed to understand what was happening on some esoteric level beyond language. They, like the others, began to advance on Marcus.

Things were getting too far out of hand. He had to prove his devotion to them all.

"I do everything for Mario and Mario alone, damn you!" Marcus ripped off his tank top and threw it to the floor. "Look at my tattoo! Do *you* have one?"

Tim lifted his left pant leg to show a Mario tattoo. "Sure do, buddy. Got Luigi on the other."

This man—this *Goomba*—could not best him.

"How about Mario underwear, then?" Marcus shouted. "I wear it! Hell, I *make* it!" He fumbled with the waistband of his pants. "Want proof?"

"What are you?" Tim spat. "Some kind of fag?"

"Ha, you don't wear it because you're not a big enough fan!" He dropped his pants. "But look at—!"

Tim lashed out with his fist, which connected solidly with Marcus' jaw. Unprepared, Marcus was slammed against the glowing Mario Head. He slid down it to the floor.

The Goomba was on him in seconds, stomping him.

Being attacked by a Goomba was the ultimate public humiliation. Too embarrassed to fight back, all Marcus could do was curl up in a ball and shield his face, feeling smaller and smaller until he imagined he could slip between the floorboards.

Suddenly, an angry voice:

"Stop it, both of you!"

The Goomba stepped back. Marcus looked up. It was Ronnie, now alongside his friend and housemate. Marcus had forgotten the other man's name, but that worried him less than the rage-filled looks that twisted the hosts' faces.

"What the hell are you doing?" shouted Ronnie's friend.

"The fucker came on to me!" screamed Tim.

"No, I didn't! I was just—"

Ronnie stamped his foot. "Sorry it had to be this way," he said, "but you gave us no choice." Both Ronnie and his friend cupped their hands around their mouths and, in a single thundering voice, shouted, "Guards!"

A door in the hallway burst open. Three men as big as Marcus proceeded into the room. They were dressed as Bowsers and had real-looking axes strapped across their chests. Partygoers pointed accusatory fingers at Marcus and Tim. The guards stalked up to them.

Marcus didn't have time to pull his pants up before a guard trapped him in a headlock and dragged him toward the hallway.

Tim, in the same predicament, shrieked, "Where are they taking us?"

"To the king!" Ronnie replied.

* * *

Musclebound Mario sprinted across the length of a bridge. Airborne Cheep Cheeps arose from beneath the bridge in an attempt to smash into him. Their efforts were futile, but he admired their spirit. Unlike Bloopers, they didn't give up once he'd exited the water world.

Just as he began a long jump from one bridge to another, the sky darkened. But the sun always went down between certain levels, not during them. The inconsistency threw him off his game so much that he almost botched the landing.

Once on the other bridge, he couldn't get a proper footing. Looking down, he realized it was because the floor of this bridge was slick with ice.

Musclebound Mario stumbled about. Just in time, he noticed a white thing—like a squat, deformed snowman—that slid toward him. He hopped over it quickly and took a backwards glance. It was a Flurry from *Super Mario Bros. 2.*

Spinning in the other direction, he saw a Clawgrip walking sideways, clacking one pincher while gripping a boulder in the other.

For the first time, Musclebound Mario felt something other than bliss. His stomach rolled. Hands quivered. He had little experience with enemies not found in the first *Super Mario Bros.* game.

The Clawgrip tossed its boulder. Musclebound Mario jumped, avoided it, but plowed headfirst into a soaring Cheep Cheep. He didn't need to hear the sound effect to know that he had shrunk.

I wish I was home, he thought. But that made no sense. He *was* home.

He heard something overhead. Looking up, it seemed to him that the entire night sky was filled with colorful dots. Cheep Cheeps forgotten, he watched the dots become a host of villains, swooping down from the stars.

Pidgets on magic flying carpets dive-bombed him. Albatrosses lobbed explosives that detonated all around his feet. Laiktus, ensconced in clouds, rained Spineys upon his head.

Musclebound Mario jumped to the third bridge. Here, Beezos charged at him with tridents outstretched, Pansers puked balls of fire and Cobrats shot up from holes in the ice like zombies from their graves.

Above him, the sun reappeared with an angry face and came alive. It plummeted in an arc. Struck Musclebound Mario in the face. All he could do was ignore the burning pain and run faster, even as he traveled atop an unbroken line of Purcupos, their quills shredding the soles of his boots.

He neared the end of the bridge, prepared to jump, but stopped at the very edge. The space between the two spans was too wide for him to cross.

His enemies saw that he was trapped. They formed a cloud around him. Beezos stabbed. Cobrats bit. Firesnakes burned.

A Birdo launched an egg. Musclebound Mario jumped atop it and was carried away. Land-based villains stood helplessly on the bridge, but Albatrosses and Laiktus still dropped their payloads while the Angry Sun circled the sky.

He jumped off the egg once it reached a ledge. There was no flagpole, just a tiny opening in a cliff face. Beyond it, he saw Firebars, hundreds if not thousands of them, lining a black and narrow hall.

His chest was sunken. His arms and legs were sticks. Still, he couldn't turn back. He had to trust his body, so he jumped headlong into darkness.

After passing the first Firebar, he turned to see that his attackers had all stopped by the entranceway. Hope restored, he bounded confidently over obstacles. He would, no doubt, make it out of this strange level alive.

Then a Phanto mask dropped down from the ceiling. With an invidious grin, it zigzagged across the hall and plowed repeatedly into his back and chest.

Musclebound Mario caught sight of a pipe. It was close, but The Phanto was relentless. He didn't know how much smaller it could make him before he shrank to nothing at all.

* * *

Marcus was led with his attacker through the same door from which the guards had exited. He found himself in a pitch-black room. Either there were no windows, or they were covered in heavy curtains.

"Keep moving," a guard behind him said, and prodded him with an axe.

They stopped in the center of what felt like a huge chamber. Suddenly, two spotlights came on—harsh and glaring. One illuminated his group, the other something directly in front of it.

Marcus squinted. At first, all he could see was a blob. Seconds later, that blob resolved itself into a man dressed as Mario—except wearing a crown instead of a hat—enthroned in a golden, bejeweled chair. Though the chair was clearly wood, the jewels clearly plastic, the effect was awe-inspiring because the man—the *king*—appeared exactly how Marcus visualized Mario, were Mario a creature of flesh and blood. Tawny skin. Big moustache like a brush. Wide, staring blue eyes. His body, all squares and stair-like edges, had been surgically modified to appear pixilated.

The king's devotion was incredible. Marcus had to bow.

"Arise, you cur!" the king growled. "Arise and pull up your pants!"

Marcus did as he was told. "How did you get—?" he started to ask.

A guard prodded him with the butt of his axe. "Be quiet! The king is preparing to speak!"

The king sat back and laced together nail-free fingers, each with only one joint. He seemed to think for a while. Finally, in a voice booming and stentorian, he said, "Timothy, I am very disappointed in you. You've attended these gatherings for years. I thought you knew and understood the rules."

The Goomba hung his head.

"You cannot fight people here, or elsewhere. Only in games. That, Timothy, is the secret to happiness and world peace."

Tim's voice was barely a whisper. "I know, and I have failed you."

"Yes. Yes, you have." The king turned his attention to Marcus. "And you. You're the one who only likes the first *Super Mario Bros.* game."

"Yes, your majesty. I just think—"

"Silence! I don't care what *you* think. *I* think you're a silly, silly man!"

"But—"

"No, buts! I've been fully briefed." He patted a cell phone. "I know what you've done out there. I know how you've vexed my most loyal subjects. I even know about your unfortunate… erection."

Marcus wanted to wilt.

"But your most grievous crime was sowing discord and violence in what should have been a peaceful gathering of likeminded souls."

"I didn't lay a hand on the Goomba!" Marcus protested. "I was only trying to show him—"

"I'm not asking for a rebuttal! I'm telling you the way things are…"

The king droned on, but Marcus' attention had shifted elsewhere. He'd been so focused on the king's appearance and defending himself that he hadn't noticed the woman lying in a coil by the base of the throne. Her head was down, hands hidden beneath her stomach, and, at first glance, she appeared to be nothing more than a bundle of gauzy fabric.

Maybe she sensed him staring at her, for, at that moment, she lifted her likewise crowned and pixilated head.

Marcus gasped. *The Princess.*

Though she looked straight at him, he doubted she

saw him. Her stare was vacant, like her body was there but her mind, elsewhere.

"Is she okay?" Marcus asked.

The king's face reddened. "No more interruptions! Listen as I speak, for this is important!" He drew a long breath. "As I was saying, all Mario games are created equal, imbued by their creator with…"

Again, Marcus tuned him out. He couldn't stop thinking about the Princess, how lost she seemed, and how her empty expression looked out-of-place above the ornate bead and lacework of her pink and billowy dress.

He had to know what troubled her. "Princess, I—"

The king slammed square fists upon the armrests of his throne. "You are not to address her! I alone have that privilege!"

"If the Princess is with Mario, she should be happy." He looked down again. Tried and failed to catch her gaze. "But she's so sad."

"What do you know about her happiness?" the king contested. "She is *my* princess! I saved her, so now I can do with her whatever I please!" His gaze met the woman's. His lips, altered to appear as though part of his moustache, parted and he said, "Blow me."

"Yes, your highness," she replied, her voice a monotone.

Marcus watched in horror as she slid onto the king's lap, unzipped his fly and reached a delicate, seemingly 8-bit hand into his pants.

He swatted her hand. "That won't be necessary, my love. I was just proving a point." He glared at Marcus, attempted a smirk. "Was the point made?"

Marcus seethed. Turning the Princess from a thing of eternal beauty into a mere sex toy was an act of abomination. "Who the hell made a man like you king?" he demanded.

"The universe, of course. It was meant to be."

Marcus made fists. He couldn't believe he'd bowed to this monster. The king had transformed himself but was still a pretender, forever unworthy of his title. "I won't stand—" he said before a guard prodded him, this time in the ribs.

"You will stand whenever I tell you to stand!" He returned his attention to the Princess. "As for you, please return to your customary spot."

She resumed her place below the throne, bowing her head to stare at the floor. Though the Princess said nothing, Marcus knew that she wanted him to save her, to lift her up from this pit and into the light of day. "I can't let you disrespect—" he began.

"We're through discussing the Princess!" The king's voice became dark, gravelly. "I am now ready to pronounce my judgment upon you both."

The room began to feel more like a basement, or a crypt. Marcus' hands and feet tingled.

The king stood. "You both have stained Mario's honor and glory in your mockery of a gathering held in his honor." He pointed at the Goomba. "Timothy, you are to wear the Mark of Shame for the duration of this party and thereafter be banished for an entire year." Then he pointed at Marcus. "You—what's your name again?"

"Marcus!"

"Well then, Marcus, due to your insolence and unthinkable devotion to a single game in the Mario Bros. cannon, your banishment is *permanent*. Never shall you step foot here again!"

"That's not right! I—"

"You will let me finish!"

Marcus bowed his head. He felt chastised by this man and hated himself for it.

"Nor are you to contact anyone you've met here today. The veil of silence is upon you forevermore!" With that, the king sat back down, sighed loudly and unleashed a fart.

He looked so smug, sitting there. Marcus wanted to punch that smugness out the back of his head. "You can't do this!" he shouted. "Don't you understand? I've finally found—"

"I will hear no more! My decision is final!"

"No, I won't—"

"It's *final*!" He waved a dismissive hand. "Be gone from my sight!"

Again, the guards seized both men. Marcus tried to get another look at the Princess, perhaps say something to her, but they poked him with axes, poked him in the stomach and ribs, poked him right out the door, right through the party where everyone could see his expulsion, and poked him right out the house to his car.

* * *

Musclebound Mario shot from the pipe into a water world. Quickly, he spun around, expecting his pursuer to give chase. How could a little water stop a possessed mask that wasn't supposed to be in this game?

But no, it hovered at the mouth of the tunnel, seeming to watch him.

He imagined he shouldn't question a blessing. After so much horror, it was nice to be back in the water, and the level looked exactly like the one he'd left in World 2-2. Never had he felt happier to see Bloopers and Cheep Cheeps in their pink, coral-filled home.

Now, all he needed to do was find a mushroom. Get big. There were no mushrooms hidden here.

He aimed to hurry past this level—the longer he remained small, the less real he felt—but his wasted arms and legs only allowed him to swim so fast, and aquatic enemies seemed suddenly formidable. He gave them wide berths and didn't dare punch them, much less turn back flips or do anything else that might open him up to their attacks.

He entered the pipe, exhausted. His body twisted like a rag doll through it. So weak, he doubted he'd be able to jump over the stairs to the flagpole. He'd have to crawl up them, fall down the other side, and take the flag from ground level. Few points were earned that way, and no glory—but it was preferable to giving up or dying.

The pipe spat him out, not at a flagpole, but, again, at the start of World 2-2.

Instantly, he understood what had happened, where he was, but he didn't want to believe it. Realization alone had numbed him.

The Phanto hadn't followed him in because it already had him where it wanted him. Through a backdoor, it had led him into Minus World—a glitch level in an otherwise perfect game.

Stuck in a recursive loop, all Musclebound Mario could do was wait for the timer to wind down to zero, wait to die.

And what if there was no re-start for him? Then the Princess would never escape her dark dungeon, would never thank him and kiss him, would never marry him and father all of his children, who'd grow up to be big and strong. And the universe would darken, as there'd be no heroes left in it.

The water level—once his favorite place in this or any other world—had become the burial vault for his body and his dreams.

Musclebound Mario sank to the bottom of the pool and wept.

* * *

Back at his apartment, Marcus looked at his reflection in the bathroom mirror, at the dark circles under his eyes, at the scruff on his face and the yellow gunk beneath his nose. It had taken all his willpower to not drive his car over a bridge or into a wall of oncoming traffic, just to see what it felt like to die.

"You're a stupid son of bitch," he said to his reflection. "You think you look so good, but you look like shit."

His reflection said nothing. It stared back at him with dumb, meathead eyes. Marcus poked them with his fingers, stubbing the digits against glass.

"You have nothing. You *are* nothing."

When his reflection remained mute, he beat his head against the mirror until he felt no pain. Glaring past red streaks, he gave it a wide, shit-eating grin.

"Ha! Serves you right, you fucker! The Princess was in the same room—and you just stood there!"

Suddenly, there was a muffled voice.

"Oh, now you decide to talk!" Again, he slammed his head against his reflection.

After the third strike, the voice returned. He realized it wasn't coming from the mirror, but couldn't find its source.

The voice sounded clearer now that he wasn't banging his head. "Come here," it said. "Please."

Whatever it was, it was in the living room.

Marcus staggered into the hall like a drunk, dripping blood on shag carpeting. When he reached the living room, he found it empty.

"Closer." The voice sounded Japanese, and it seemed inside the TV.

The TV was off.

"Please," the voice continued. "I have much to tell you."

No, it wasn't inside the TV, but in the picture of Shigeru Miyamoto atop it. The Creator, Marcus realized, had addressed him personally.

And the sugar cookie once on the plate below was gone.

"Mr. Miyamoto?" he said.

"Yes, of course," said the cheerful-looking, lank haired Asian man from his frame.

"I—I don't know what to say! This is an honor! A blessing!"

Mr. Miyamoto's right arm, which had never before been visible, beckoned him forward. "Again, Marcus, please come closer."

"You know my name? And you see me?"

"Of course. I see everything from where I stand."

"But where are you?"

"Here."

"I know, but—"

"Don't ask so many questions, please. Just listen."

Marcus got as close as he could to the picture without feeling that he was infringing on Mr. Miyamoto's personal space.

"I've watched you play my game for years," the Creator continued. "It's a pleasure to finally speak with you, one-on-one."

"Oh, I agree! 100%!"

His tone deepened. "But I can't help but notice that you look down, and your head is a total mess."

Marcus felt self-conscious. He went to clean his face with his shirt before remembering that he'd torn it off at the party.

"Tell me, what's gone wrong?"

He didn't want to say anything, didn't want to reveal his personal failings. But Mr. Miyamoto's face was so kind, so loving, so beneficent and all knowing. He simply couldn't conceal anything from him.

"Everything, Mr. Miyamoto! Finally, I find people I can connect with, and then I get banished from them! But I don't want to be alone! I want to talk with people, love them and... you know..." His cheeks went red. "...maybe even have sex."

"That's what we all want," the Creator said.

"I haven't been with a woman in so long, and I could have saved the Princess! Really, I could have I—" He couldn't look at the Creator anymore. His face fell into his hands. "I'm… I'm a bad boy."

"Wrong, Marcus. Anyone who loves my game as much as you do is a good boy, indeed."

He looked up. "You mean that?"

"Of course. Now, go get a bowl."

"I don't smoke marijuana, Mr. Miyamoto."

"Not that kind of bowl," he said. "A *regular* bowl. From your kitchen."

"Oh." Wobbly legs moved Marcus to the kitchen. There, he picked up the first bowl he saw—a big, blue one, covered in Mario and Luigi heads. He brought it into the living room, showed it to Mr. Miyamoto. "What do you want me to do with it?" he asked.

"I want you to eat the cereal."

"But I didn't get any, Mr. Miyamoto. You just told me to—"

His smile was wide. "Look down again."

To Marcus' surprise, the bowl wasn't empty at all, but filled with cereal, swimming in milk. Mario head puffs and Luigi and Princess marshmallows—*Mario Crunch* had become a reality.

"My god! And now what do I do, Mr. Miyamoto?"

"You eat."

Happily, Marcus took the first bite. It was the best cereal he'd ever tasted, so sweet and crunchy. He shoveled in another spoonful before he'd swallowed the first.

"This is a different sort of nourishment," the Creator said, "so close your eyes as you chew. Forget who you are now. Forget what happened. Get in touch with the child you once were."

Marcus obeyed and, at once, images formed in his mind.

"What do you see?"

"I see myself playing your game."

"Go beyond that. Find something you've forgotten."

Marcus' thoughts slipped past a black and white mongrel dog named Bowser, past talking about *Super Mario Bros.* with a neighbor kid—he forgot the name—to a time before he knew of the game. He saw an attic, remembered that it was in his great grandmother's house. Then, in an instant, he was no longer merely seeing it. He was crawling across the warped floorboards of this place, finding all the strange old things that were secreted up there and imagining the motes that floated listlessly in sunbeams were ghosts.

He felt as light as those motes, like gravity itself was letting go of him. There was a world outside, and people in it, but that did not concern him.

"Do you feel like a kid again?" the Creator asked.

Marcus came back to himself, but the buzz remained. "No, I am a kid again."

"Good, good. But this magic isn't permanent. If you want lasting change, you must act to create it."

He questioned these words, and the adult world crowded back in on him. He felt its weight, pressing down. "Act how?"

"That's for you to figure out. I can only guide you."

"But I don't know—"

"Think like a child!" he shouted.

Marcus wracked his brain before he realized this was the wrong approach. He had to relax, take it easy. The answer would come to him naturally.

Finally, he'd figured it out.

Marcus started off toward the bedroom, but turned back around to address the Creator. "Can I...bring you with me?"

He smiled. "Please."

Marcus grabbed up Mr. Miyamoto and brought him to the nightstand, turning his picture so the Creator could see what he was about to do. Then he punched himself hard in the mouth. His lips split, but teeth remained planted firmly in gums. He punched himself again, and a tooth fell into his free hand.

"Yes," said Mr. Miyamoto. "Yes."

For what he needed, he doubted a single tooth would suffice, so he hammered both fists against his mouth. Blood poured, and he winced, but, in less than a minute, he had three more teeth in his palm.

Marcus got down on his hands and knees, lifted his pillow and placed his bloody teeth under it. Then he removed his pants and got into bed.

"Please," said the Creator. "Take me to bed with you. I will protect you as you sleep."

Marcus took the picture from the nightstand and laid it on the covers beside him.

"Do you feel better?"

"My head and teeth hurt. But yeah, I do."

"Good. Now go to sleep, Mario. Go to sleep and dream."

"You called me Mario."

His lips started to glow, his smile suddenly iridescent. "So I did."

"But you know my name is Marcus."

"Is it really?"

Marcus wasn't sure of anything, but that didn't trouble him. He watched Mr. Miyamoto's lips continue to brighten, followed by the rest of his face and suit. The picture became Marcus' nightlight, and he never felt more warm and secure as he closed his eyes, made a wish, and drifted off to sleep.

* * *

Musclebound Mario could not curl up and embrace death. He needed to believe that the strength of his will trumped the Minus World glitch.

With this conviction firmly in mind, he dislodged stones from the sea floor and dug his hands into grit, feeling around until he happened upon something mired below. Seemed like a rock. Nevertheless, he said, "It's a flagpole," and pulled.

It hurt. Atrophied muscles threatened to pop, but still he pulled, pulled until pain diminished and his body swelled with the effort, restoring his size and physique.

He looked up at the timer. A minute remained. He had to keep pulling—keep believing—so he strained until the thing started to rise. Looking down, he saw the tip of a thick metal rod and a swath of yellow fabric. The sight invigorated him, and with a sudden and powerful yank, he exhumed an entire flagpole.

He seized the flag and swam away, plunging his fists *through* Bloopers and Cheep Cheeps whenever they dared approach. He hurried past the bottomless pit and pink coral and slid into a pipe.

PART TWO:
MUSCLEBOUND MARIO

From the pipe, he was expelled into a bright world of flat-topped trees of varying heights. He didn't care that the next level should have been another bridge, replete with flying fish. He had defeated the Minus World and its evil glitch.

Musclebound Mario bounded past treetop after treetop, his massive body able to land upon without breaking even the most delicate branch. He hardly noticed the enemies that mulled about the level. They posed no threat. The only real danger was miscalculating a jump.

Not that he would ever do that.

Halfway through the level, the villains ceased to move. Glancing down as he soared far above the tree line, Musclebound Mario noticed that their bodies seemed somehow different too.

He landed upon the closest tree. Confusion segued into near horror as a line of villains presented itself to him.

A Koopa Troopa—three heads bristling from a bright pink, graffiti-covered shell—stood between a purple, flower-sprouting Spiney and a squished yet still-living Goomba. Beside the Goomba was a molten conglomeration of so many villains that Musclebound Mario couldn't begin to classify it.

They all stared at him, eyes dark and empty like holes in dirt.

He bounced into the air and came back down again. They did not react.

"Come on!" he challenged. "Attack me!"

As one, their mouths opened. Something like the wind came out. Then a single monotone voice wafted from their throats. "We see nothing," the voice said. "We are lost and cannot be found."

Musclebound Mario took a step back. "You talk?"

"We know not what we do."

"You're not supposed to do that!" He groaned. "What the hell?"

"We cannot know ourselves. We are no more. We may never be again."

The weight of their collective, unblinking stares devastated his nerves. "Stop fucking staring!" he shouted.

At that moment, stares deepened until black holes became vortexes. They swirled and churned, threatening to suck him up and into them. He had to avert his gaze. "Just be normal, damn it!"

Instead, his enemies began to chant in a harsh, guttural tongue.

Musclebound Mario slammed his hands to his ears but still heard the sound. His jaw tightened; he felt the hard rush of blood in his veins. Lashing out, he stomped the already-stomped Goomba, blew fire on the conglomerate and punted the pink Koopa Troopa high into the sky.

Behind him, there was a noise like crackling cellophane. He turned. An oval-shaped patch of air at the tree's edge shone and shimmered before becoming a portal. Within it, a dark and hulking shadow resolved itself. Red mohawked hair, green scaly skin and turtle-shell back that bristled with horns, Bowser was nude except for twin metal-studded leather wristbands.

Musclebound Mario didn't question the villain's

arrival. Fists up and knees bent, he went into immediate defense mode.

But Bowser spat no fireballs and threw no axes. He stood there, looking out at the world with eyes that smoldered, smoke rising in gray plumes from his nostrils.

"Not you, too!" Musclebound glanced behind the villain but saw no axe-shaped lever. Clueless how to proceed, and in a blind fury, he ran up to Bowser, punched his face and kicked his shins. "I will fuck you up, you fucker!" he shouted.

"Woah! Woah!" Bowser held up both claws. "Hold on!"

He discharged a fireball. "Never!"

"Seriously, stop! I need to talk to you!"

"Lies!" He tugged at Bowser's mohawk. "And you're not supposed to talk!"

Bowser's roar rattled branches beneath their feet. "Damn it! I said, *stop!*"

Against his better judgment, Musclebound Mario pulled back. As Bowser caught his breath, the hero spotted a small, worm-like appendage that dangled from the villain's groin.

"You have a dick!" he shouted.

"I know, but—"

"And you shouldn't even be here! Get back in your dungeon!"

"If you'd let me—"

"Stop trying to explain shit!" Musclebound Mario adopted an attack stance. "Fight me, you son of a bitch!" Again, he charged.

Bowser outstretched his arm, deflecting Musclebound Mario and nearly hurtling him from the tree. Falling hard on his ass, the hero squirmed a bit before he managed to sit upright.

Bowser looked down at him. Shook his head. "Don't you get it? I *can't* fight you."

"What do you mean, *you can't*? It's your job!"

"It was my job to fight Mario and Luigi, not you."

"But I'm the hero!"

"No, you're an interloper."

Quickly, Musclebound Mario arose and stalked up to Bowser. "You'd better take that back!"

"I'm afraid I can't."

"I'm afraid *you will*! I was doing everything right until this shit started!" He looked to the flower-sprouting Spiney and the eternally staring villains perched on the nearest tree. "What the hell is wrong with those assholes?"

"You're what's wrong with them," Bowser said, "and what's wrong with me." He turned. A deformed parasitic twin the size of an infant hung loathsomely from his left flank. Jaws clattered up and down. Claws dug at the scabs and tumors that riddled its body.

"Please!" Musclebound Mario cried. "Turn back around!"

Bowser acquiesced. "So you see, much has changed, and it will continue to change—unless *you* do something about it."

Musclebound Mario's stomach still roiled. "Okay, okay! I'll save the Princess!" He kicked at leaves and huffed. "That's what I was doing before you guys got weird on me."

Bowser's voice deepened. "The nature of the quest has changed, I'm afraid."

He bristled. He didn't like the thought of change.

"It's not a princess that needs saving, but a *prince*."

The hero felt as though he'd been gut punched. "I don't save Princes!" he shouted. "Princes save themselves!"

"But you *must* save him. If you do not—"

Musclebound Mario stamped his foot. The entire tree was jolted. "No! This is stupid, and I won't do it!"

"Listen to me. There's—"

"I said I refuse!"

"Try to—"

"No, I want to go back to the game!"

Bowser clomped over to him, the smoke from his nostrils now coal-black. "Interrupt me one more time, and I might do something we'll both regret."

The hero puffed out his substantial chest, mustered up all his confidence, tilted his chin to the sky and said, "I can take whatever you've got."

Bowser's face contorted with rage, eyes like slits, lips flared out and curling. Seizing Musclebound Mario by his plumber's shirt, he pulled him up against a cold, scaly body. Perspective made the villain's nostrils appear as big as saucers.

His voice was a terrible roar. "Fucking listen to me or die!"

Musclebound Mario recoiled, first at the roar and then at the smell of Bowser's breath. It washed over him, smelling of old socks, rotten eggs and cat shit. "You have no right to refuse!" the villain shrieked. "You're a virus! Because of you, our world crumbles!"

Musclebound Mario said nothing to this. He didn't know what to say. Things suddenly seemed very real to him, everything vivid and sparkling with danger.

Bowser formed a fist the size of a ham hock. "Believe me, I'd love to see you die like Mario or Luigi, impaled by my axes or burned by my fire. I'd love to see your corpse crisp in the molten lake under my bridge. But you're the only one who can help, so get your ass out there and do what's right!"

Saliva fell onto Musclebound Mario's head in hot ropes. "Okay, dude! Okay! Just chill out!"

Bowser took a step back from the hero. Following a deep breath and a moment of silence, he said, "If you do nothing, our world will be lost. You don't want that, do you?"

"Of course not!"

"Then go and save that Prince!"

It soured his stomach, the thought of taking orders from Bowser, but his concern for the game overrode all others. "Will I have to…kiss him?" he asked.

"Only if you want," Bowser said.

Serenaded by birdsong—*Why are fucking birds here?* Musclebound Mario wanted to scream—the duo bounced toward and atop tree after tree. Was this yet another recursive level? The hero looked up for the timer but saw it nowhere in the sky.

On what had to be the thousandth tree, villains had merged into one massive yet useless-looking super-villain. It regarded Musclebound Mario with a dozen eyes and spurted green ooze from a flabby, hole-ridden body.

He stomped it to end its misery.

With no real enemies to confront, it was easy to imagine his legs as pumping pistons and space out. Still, Musclebound Mario snuck a furtive glance at Bowser. The villain wasn't about to try anything, so he blanked his mind again.

When he spaced back in, he saw how the green leaves had shifted, without him realizing it, to red, orange and gold. The colors were evocative and brought to mind thoughts of riding bikes, playing with small balls of various sizes and colors and building castles in boxes full of sand— all experiences he couldn't have possibly lived.

How long had he phased out, he wondered. Then he looked at Bowser. The villain seemed to be in the same reflective mode. "What are you thinking about?" he asked him.

"Defeating Mario, tasting his eight-bit blood and keeping the Princess all to myself," he said, dreamily.

"You really hate Mario, don't you?"

"No, not at all. I just do what's required. I raid the

Mushroom Kingdom, steal the Princess and—" Pausing, he appeared forlorn. "Guess I should have used the past tense."

The villain's sorrow seemed genuine. "I'm sorry for being a little bitch earlier," Musclebound Mario said, an attempt to lighten the mood between them.

"Whatever. It's fine."

"But really, I—"

"I said *whatever*! It's fine!"

Chastised, Musclebound Mario looked down at his feet. There, he saw that the leaves were no longer gold, but a dark and dirty brown, and the birds were but bones in their nests. Immediately, his thoughts churned over to gloomier subjects, to sickness, death and graveyards.

Before he could jump, there was a rumble followed by a harsh *snap*. That *snap*, he realized, was the sound of the lifeless tree, breaking in half.

The plunge was quick and violent. As he tumbled, Musclebound Mario looked down and saw nothing but thin air and the ground so far below. Though it made him feel weak, he grabbed onto Bowser's right arm and clung tightly to it.

They landed hard, but Musclebound Mario arose within seconds. He crouched defensively. His head swiveled back and forth. His eyes scanned for threats.

Bowser remained on the ground. Grimacing, he clutched his left shin. "My leg's broken!" he cried. "You're going to have to carry me!"

"What? That's crazy talk! I can't do that!"

"Why not?"

"*Because you're my sworn enemy!*"

Tears streamed from red, squinty eyes. "Oh god, it hurts!"

"Please don't do that. Don't cry."

"If you want me to stop, then pick me up!"

"I told you, I can't do that!"

"But you must!"

"No! No! No!"

As they argued, a tree whose branches hung over them began to teeter, black leaves falling from skeletal branches like rain.

"Hurry!" Bowser shouted.

Musclebound Mario grumbled, but he couldn't let something as stupid as a tree take out Bowser. Cradling the villain in his arms, he ran out of its path.

At once, all dead trees started to fall, crashing down like angry hands trying to crush bugs. A maze of obstacles was formed. As Musclebound Mario hopped, slid, dove and ran, he felt a chill, not due to the trees, but due to the subtle gleam in Bowser's eyes and the way he flashed his teeth and licked his lips when he looked up at him.

Past the gauntlet, Musclebound Mario tried to orient himself, but the world beyond the trees was benighted and felt colder than any ice level. He heard a series of hums, backed by a sound akin to static. The hero had no idea what was creating this before a luminescent insect lighted on his arm and produced the same sound.

In a short time, the already dark sky blackened until it seemed that even the glow of the insects had been extinguished.

Still, the duo pressed on. They traveled uphill. Then, suddenly, they traveled downhill. It felt like they were in water up to their necks then, almost as quickly, on platforms that moved up and down and side-to-side. Something else—a giant trebuchet, perhaps—flung them far into the night. They landed in what had to be quicksand and struggled to break free.

It was all so disorienting. Musclebound Mario didn't know whether to walk or swim or jump. Confused and blinded, he walked straight into a brick wall, slamming his outstretched arms, and Bowser, hard against it.

"Sorry about that," he said.

"Put me down," said the villain.

"I already said I was sorry!"

"Just do as I say, alright?"

Musclebound Mario obeyed, and Bowser leapt up so high that he became like a dot superimposed over a void and then like nothing at all. Minutes passed before the hero heard him return to earth on the other side of the wall.

Musclebound Mario bounded over and joined him there. "You faker!" he fumed. "You didn't break your leg!"

There was an unseen grin. "So I didn't."

"And you were showing off! There's no way in hell you needed to jump that high!"

"If you can mess so hard with my day," Bowser stated, matter-of-factly, "then I can make you carry me around a bit."

Musclebound Mario granted that he had a point, but still felt used.

For hours, they stumbled and staggered. Then Bowser said, "Let us sleep. We're not going to see anything until the night ends, provided it ends at all."

Though Musclebound Mario never recalled sleeping, he somehow knew what it was, and it seemed like a great idea. He was so tired even his bones ached.

In the darkness, one dry and stationary spot was as good as the other. Once settled down, the hero turned to the all-but-invisible villain. "So," he asked, "what's the first level going to be like?"

Bowser shrugged. "How should I know?"

"What do you mean, *how should I know*? Aren't you supposed to be my guide?"

"This is as new to me as it is to you."

"Just tell me—"

"Look, I already told you everything I know."

"But—"

"Remember who started all this, okay. I didn't have a will before you showed up."

"Listen, man, you can't blame this on me!"

Squinting, Bowser focused his gaze on something. "Be quiet!" he hissed.

"Sheesh! What crawled up your—"

"I said *be quiet!*"

Musclebound Mario opened his mouth, again to complain, but then he saw it, too. Something dark and inky in the near distance. Something that slunk like an encroaching animal. A large dog, perhaps. He could see it only as an outline somehow blacker than the air around it. Body appearing to hitch in laughter, it projected its energy at them and made the whole world feel like a room in which something bad had happened.

And then, as quickly as it had arrived, it was gone. "What the hell was that?" Musclebound Mario demanded.

"The thing you'll fight and hopefully vanquish, I'd guess," said Bowser.

Musclebound Mario didn't like monsters that were unfamiliar to him. "*Thing*? *You'd guess*? Don't you know what it is?"

"All I know is that it isn't good."

"Hell, I could have told you that!"

Bowser laid a scaly yet reassuring claw on Musclebound Mario's shoulder. "Don't worry. Maybe it's just trying to scare you."

He didn't like "maybes," either. He liked certainties, some more so than others. Like a Goomba will always be in a certain place at a certain time and that 12 coins will always be in the third pot in World 3-1.

Nearly a minute later, Bowser still gripped him with his claw.

"You can take your hand off me whenever," the hero said, voice wavering.

Slowly, the claw slid away.

Sleep claimed them both, and Musclebound Mario dreamt of the dark thing he'd seen. It slipped in from underneath a door and shared an otherwise empty room with him. Still a shadow, it throbbed as it expanded to fill the space around him and seemed like not one, but a million different entities. Then the thing filled him, too.

In time, night became morning, and the hero awoke with no memory of the dream.

He looked around at a world he could finally see. Hills were up in the sky. Clouds were on the ground. A collection of broken bridges, platforms and pulleys that should never share the same level were heaped in the air above him. The pots of Piranha Plants were upside down and covered with obscene graffiti—Goombas being gang raped by Koopa Troopas and vice versa. Plants inside shook the pots and screamed for freedom. Musclebound Mario felt a tug of guilt for not saving them, but knew they would try to eat him if he did.

This is the Mushroom Kingdom, he thought and wanted to sigh. He alone was responsible for its current state. Though this fact strengthened his resolve to make things right, it failed to stoke his enthusiasm for saving the Prince.

He looked over at Bowser, who slumbered. "Hey," he said. "Wake up."

Still, he snored.

Musclebound Mario scooted to the villain and began to shake him. Lids concealing yellow, blood-shot eyes flew open. A claw arose, wrapped around the hero's neck and squeezed.

"I'll rip your dick off and shove it in *my* mouth! I'll—" he started, then, "Oh, it's you."

"Yes, you asshole!" he choked, eyes bulging. "It's me!"

"Well…never startle me like that!" He loosened his grip on the hero's throat but did not let go. "What the hell were you doing?"

"Trying to wake you!"

"Well, don't do it again!"

"Don't worry, I won't!"

The villain released him. "I'm sorry, okay. You fucked things up, but you're still the hero." He broke eye contact. "I must remind myself of that, always."

"Please do," Musclebound Mario said, heart pounding hard, nerves frazzled. It didn't help things when Bowser turned slightly, and the hero once again saw the fetal twin joined to his flank.

Once both hero and villain had calmed sufficiently, they got up to begin their day.

After a few steps, a metal bar fell from the sky and impacted the ground by Musclebound Mario's feet. A few more steps, and he slid in a puddle. *Water*, he thought, but then realized it was the liquefied remains of a Koopa Troopa. The smell of sweet, sticky rot hit his nose. Scowling, he wiped his shoes clean on dead grass.

"This sucks," he said.

"Tell me about it," Bowser replied.

Musclebound Mario and Bowser bounded over bridges that had been built flush with the ground, through tainted green water filled with Blooper and Cheep Cheep skeletons and across ice patches in otherwise blistering heat where cacti and pyramids were entombed.

The hero began to bore. He didn't like that there was nothing to shoot at, jump upon or kill. If this was his quest, then it was a stupid one.

Past a castle that was a cardboard prop held up by 2x4s, they caught sight of a massive green Piranha Plant pot. Unlike everything else in the world, it was oriented correctly and appeared as it should.

A single long jump brought them to the pot. There, Musclebound Mario studied the thing as though doing so might cause it to spill its secrets. Then he turned to Bowser. "What do we do now?" he asked.

The villain grinned. "You should have said *what do I do now?*"

"You mean you can't come along? Not even on the first level?"

Bowser shook his head. "I am powerless to save the Prince. As I said, Musclebound Mario, you alone are able."

He'd assumed they'd be a tag team like the old Mario and Luigi. He sighed with resignation. Then it struck him as odd that he might feel safer in the presence of a villain. Maybe he was growing accustomed to the guy.

"Are you *sure* sure?" he pressed.

"Sorry," Bowser commiserated. "That's just the way it is."

"Okay. But it's a bummer, you know."

"Maybe I can make it up to you someday."

Perhaps, Musclebound Mario thought, he could make it up to him now. "Can I at least get your autograph?" He stammered a bit. "Later, I mean"—though he wanted it immediately—"at the end of the quest."

"We'll see."

"Okay, but I'd really appreciate it if—"

Before he could finish, there was a creaking sound. He turned to see the pot's hard shell soften as its mouth swelled into lips that puckered and flapped. Thin, ropy arms sprouted from all sides and whipped the air like mad vines.

Lips flaring, the Piranha in the pot grew an eye and

glared down at Musclebound Mario. He lost control of his bladder when it lunged and, in a single gulp, swallowed him whole.

He found himself inside a warm, moist tube, nothing but sticky darkness and the smell of raw meat around him. With muscular contractions, the pot forced his body farther down as though it were being processed inside of an intestine.

PART THREE:
UNCONVENTIONAL CONVENTIONIST

He was shat out in the middle of the dealer's room of a fan convention.

Conventioneers milled about the room. Some snapped pictures. Others stretched their necks over cases, humming and hawing, while still others held animated conversations amongst themselves or simply stood, staring vacantly as though they had trouble connecting with others or deciding where to begin.

Musclebound Mario felt uncomfortable amongst things that weren't originally eight-bit. Still, he moved purposely toward the exit as conventioneers and their conversations swirled:

"Do you already have that poster?"

"No, and it's mine! Don't even look at it!"

"Is this a first edition?"

"Fucking idiot, can't you tell it's a second edition?"

"God, I wish I could wear his skin!"

"We all do, man. We all do."

Musclebound Mario took notice of a particular conventioneer, admiring something in one of the cases. The man's back was turned to him, so he could not see his face. He could, however, hear squelchy sounds. Peering past the man, he saw that the case dripped with gallons of jizz.

The hero turned away quickly and strayed into the path of another conventioneer.

"Oh hey! Sorry, dude!" he said, gaze aimed at the conventioneer's chest to avoid eye contact. He noticed the man wore a laminated pin on his shirt. Musclebound Mario's own head provided its central image. Black text above his hair spelled out, *Weekend Pass*.

"No problem," the conventioneer replied "And great costume, by the way. I have one just like it, but it's at the cleaners."

"This?" He pulled at his overalls. "It isn't a costume."

"Of course it is, but it's pretty great. For a second there, I thought you were—" The conventioneer's expression shifted slightly as he fell silent.

Too late, Musclebound Mario realized he'd said the worst possible thing.

"No. It can't be." The conventioneer scrutinized him. "Is that really you?" He slapped both hands against his face. "It *is* you! It really is!"

"No, it really isn't. I—"

"Yes! Yes, it is!" the man called out, flailing, screaming, pointing. "It's him! It's Musclebound Mario!"

Then the lights dimmed. A spotlight focused on him as a banner emblazoned with his name and image unfurled from the ceiling. Throughout the room, headshots rolled down from tabletops and walls. One photo, above the exit, was life-sized and in a golden frame.

"Look!" someone said. "They've made it official!"

"It's him," said the entire crowd, first as a whisper then as a scream. "It's him!"

A fat woman, clasping her handbag in one hand and waving a handkerchief in the other, ran at him, a look of rapture splitting her face. "Oh Jesus," she wailed "Oh sweet Jesus!"

An elderly vendor crawled across his table,

pronounced erection in his pants. He scrambled over and punched competing vendors, many of whom punched back in their attempt to reach Musclebound Mario first.

And then everyone else in the room joined them, moving faster than mere humans should move.

"You can't have him!" someone shouted.

"Stop pushing!" said another.

But everyone was talking at the same time. Together, their voices sounded like an encroaching tide. Then the crowd itself became a wave that surged toward and engulfed him.

"Sign this!" said a man, holding a comic.

"Then sign these!" said a woman, lifting her blouse.

He smelled their collective odor until his nose bent hard against a conventioneer's chest and he stopped breathing. Rearing back his head, he gasped, "Please, I need air!"

"You need *us!*" they countered.

Conventioneers piled atop his body and forced it to the ground. Suddenly, a penis, long and lumpy, was pointed at his face. Its owner tried to insert the organ into Musclebound Mario's mouth through the wall of clamoring conventioneers.

The hero seized the arm closest to him and yanked it off. First, he used it as a wedge. Then, he used it as a battering ram. He felt numb, but didn't have time to entertain emotions. The crowd was reforming. Musclebound Mario turned from it and sprinted toward the exit door.

He threw it open with a feeling like elation. That feeling was ephemeral, for the exit led into an almost identical dealer's room. The hungry and insatiable people inside it were already running his way, their teeth elongating and sharpening into points.

Musclebound Mario dove beneath a dealer's table. There, concealed by a tablecloth, he coiled himself into a tight and hopefully impenetrable ball. In the past, he'd gotten thrills from playing the game, but never pants-shitting terror. He hadn't signed up for this. To hell with the Prince! Rocking a bit, he brought his thumb to his mouth. He lowered it once he realized what he was about to do.

Seconds later, the table was flung up and tossed aside. Conventioneers amassed. So many of them now, more than it seemed the room should hold. He watched, horror mounting, as their skin darkened and bubbled. Fingers and nails lengthened and curled. Red, segmented eyes replaced human ones in each molten head as skin flaps elongated like penises that dangled not from crotches, but from faces.

Their voices were like those of snakes, were snakes capable of speech. "We want you inside us," said some.

"We want to fuck and eat you," said others.

A gnarled, warty claw reached into his overalls and wrapped around his cock, stroked it, but he felt no pleasure.

"We *will* fuck and eat you."

A talon-like nail found its way into his ass and began to wiggle. Musclebound Mario wanted to jump up, crush all of them, but the conventioneer held his dick so firmly the hero knew he'd lose it if he moved.

"You will always be part of us."

"You will never be yourself again."

Their faces were so close to his that he saw them as a blur. In it, large black holes took shape. These, he realized, were mouths, gaping wide.

The mouths would have taken him in, were it not for a well-muscled arm that plunged into the sea of bodies. The hand attached to it broke every claw that tried to reclaim him. It bashed in and ripped off heads. It pulled him from the fray.

A tall, powerful man had rescued him and found a door that opened into a hallway. That was all Musclebound Mario knew. He was being dragged away too quickly to focus on the face that bobbed in and out of his line of sight.

Soon, he realized it wasn't just him being jostled, but the hotel itself. Walls cracked. Floors buckled and split. Monsters and merchandise plummeted into the deep, dark crater that formed in the dealer's room. The pot of a Piranha Plant rose from it as they fell. It plowed into the hall and, bowing its neck, opened its fanged mouth.

The man stepped in first and pulled Musclebound Mario in after him. After some twisting and turning, swallowed but not digested, they were shat out again into the Mushroom Kingdom.

PART FOUR:
MUSCLEBOUND LUIGI

Musclebound Mario and his savior hit the ground hard. In this world, things remained in chaos and disarray—piled up and rusty, conglomerated and confused—but now bramble and ivy covered them, and they seemed less tangible, like even inanimate objects were slowly becoming ghosts.

The hero got to his feet and beheld the man in front of him. His embellished cap. His blue overalls and green shirt, draped over a chest larger and more barrel-shaped than Musclebound Mario's own. His arms that rivaled pylons. His swarthy skin and black moustache.

No, it couldn't be.

But it was.

"Oh my god! Are you—?"

Musclebound Mario stopped talking. He knew the man's identity. It was Musclebound Luigi in the flesh, and he wore a kind, caring expression on a face that seemed so very happy to see him.

They embraced in a great hug, a hug that went on and on, perhaps for days. Musclebound Mario wanted it to last forever. He was stoked that Musclebound Luigi's emotions were as powerful as his own.

Finally, Musclebound Mario was released. He stood there for a moment in awe, not certain how to continue, provided he could continue at all in the face of such immensity. With no better plan, he shouted out the first thing that came to mind: "I can't believe you're real!"

"I can't believe you're real, either!" said Musclebound Luigi.

They spent the next few seconds staring at one another. Musclebound Mario stammered, but formed no actual words.

Musclebound Luigi was more coherent. "God, I wish I had a camera!"

"Wow! Do you mean that?"

"Of course!"

Hearing this emboldened him. He felt the need to pose, but was too self-conscious. Instead, he fanned his face with his hands. The experience was utterly intense.

He made himself relax by shifting his focus to thoughts of the One True Game. Immediately, he felt calmer, more collected. Maybe now he could act normal around the man. But then he remembered that he'd forgotten to do something very important and thoughts of acting normal fled.

"Shit!" he said. "I didn't thank you for saving me back there!"

Musclebound Luigi waved him off. "All in a day's work."

"But I would've been totally lost without you."

He laughed. "I'm sure it wasn't that bad."

"No, really, it was so terrible I don't want to think about it!" Admitting this, he felt unworthy of looking at his new friend. "It would have been embarrassing to lose all my lives at the start of the quest."

Musclebound Luigi stepped closer to him. "But it's over now, my brother. You're in good hands." He smiled. "You don't mind if I call you 'brother,' do you?"

Musclebound Mario wasn't aware of ever having a brother, or, for that matter, a mother, father or any other blood relation. Still, it edified him that someone the likes of

Musclebound Luigi had called him that, so he said, "Of course not." Then he too smiled. "But only if I can call you the same."

"Need you ask?"

Again, Musclebound Mario blushed, but then heard something approach from behind. He turned and formed a fireball, which he extinguished within seconds. He'd remembered who—or what—this squat, dinosaur-like thing was. It didn't exist in the worlds that he preferred, but in debauched, later versions that he'd dared not access.

The hero regarded the hobbling creature with disgust. Its muscles, packed awkwardly on its body, were too swollen to be aesthetically pleasing. Instead, they made the thing seem top-heavy, hunchbacked. The shell on its back, weathered and worn, had cracked under the pressure they exerted. Only short, stick-like arms threaded with varicose veins were muscle-free.

"Hello," it said to Musclebound Mario and lifted a tiny green hand. "I am Musclebound Yoshi."

Musclebound Luigi slapped the thing's hand. "Speak when spoken to, asshole!"

"I know, but—"

"Shut it! Can't you see I have a guest?" He turned to Musclebound Mario. "Don't mind him. He's retarded."

"I am not!" Musclebound Yoshi rejoined. "I just want to meet your new friend!"

"I can chat a bit, if he wants," Musclebound Mario said, an attempt at being polite. In truth, he didn't want to hold a conversation with a creature that reminded him of things outside the One True Game.

"No!" Musclebound Luigi said. "Don't encourage him!"

Musclebound Yoshi jabbed the air with middle fingers thinner than twigs. Musclebound Mario blanched. He couldn't believe that this thing—this *asshole*—had disrespected such a great man.

Musclebound Luigi's face glowed red. He snapped,

"Go sit under a tree, retard!"

"But—"

"Go sit under a tree or I'll fuck you up!"

As though expecting aid or commiseration, the creature turned to Musclebound Mario.

"Just leave," said the hero.

Without another word, Musclebound Yoshi aimed his eyes at the ground, walked about ten yards and sat beneath an upside down, orange-leafed tree that grew Spineys like fruit.

Serves him right, Musclebound Mario thought.

The other man, calm now, placed a hand on the hero's shoulder. "Say, why don't we sit down and get to know each other better?"

"That sounds awesome!" But then he remembered something, and his face fell slightly. "I'm on a mission, though. I need—"

"Come now! It's been a long day. You should think of other things."

He was right. It *had* been a long day. "Maybe," Musclebound Mario said, "but I want to play the *real* game again. I can't do that—and no one else can, either—if I fuck up."

"You can do that some other time. I mean, what happened sucks and all, but we got to meet each other because of it, right?"

The hero nodded. "I guess we did."

"So, let's go somewhere more private and talk."

"Okay," he said. "Let's do it."

Musclebound Luigi turned to Musclebound Yoshi and glared. "Stay put," he shouted, "and don't you dare try to eavesdrop!"

They found a spot behind a prop castle, the words SEX DUNGEON spray-painted on it in huge red letters. Above their heads, a Firebar, affixed to nothing but air, hitched and emitted smoke as it failed to spin. Musclebound Luigi took a seat first. Musclebound Mario sat Indian-style in front of him.

"Glad we're away from that headcase," said Musclebound Luigi.

"Yeah," replied Musclebound Mario. "So, uh, what do you want to talk about?"

"Whatever you want."

Again, the hero fidgeted. Though he had so many questions that he'd wanted to ask, he had no idea where to begin, so he said, "Just—I don't know—tell me about yourself or something."

And tell him he did. The man regaled Musclebound Mario with stories of so many battles won and so many princesses saved, wooed and bedded that he had a hard time keeping names and places straight. The hero sighed inwardly. Musclebound Luigi seemed bigger and more important than he would ever be.

"God, you must be the greatest guy around!" he said. "I'm just trying to find a stupid prince. You haven't seen an *actual* castle here, have you?"

"No, nothing like that," Musclebound Luigi said.

Musclebound Mario huffed. "Figures."

"Don't be so down. What's important is that I'm here right now, with you." His tone softened. "Can I…get a little closer?"

Musclebound Mario wasn't sure such a man should get too close to him, for fear of lessening himself. "Sure," he said, finally. "If you want."

Musclebound Luigi drew nearer. "This okay, too?"

Musclebound Mario nodded.

Closer, still. They all but touched. "And this?" he asked.

"You're still fine."

"Good, because I need to get very, very close so I can tell you a secret." He smiled. "Are you ready for it?"

The hero was more than ready. "Lay it on me!" he shouted.

Musclebound Luigi leaned over him as though to whisper in his ear. Instead, he spilled something like red wine on his shirt. Musclebound Mario couldn't recall the man having a glass, or know from where or whence it might have came.

Musclebound Luigi tittered. "Oops, guess that secret will have to wait. And sorry about your shirt." He paused a beat. "You should take it off."

"I don't know. I, uh—"

"Well, I can't force you, but you really should." He leaned his face closer to Musclebound Mario's, then sniffed the air and wrinkled his nose. "Frankly, you stink."

The regular Mario never had to battle odor. Upon lifting his left arm and smelling the pit, Musclebound Mario, with some embarrassment, realized he did.

"But don't worry. I stink, too." Musclebound Luigi clasped Musclebound Mario's shoulder. "Come, let's wash up in the lake." Suddenly, a small but inviting lake appeared in a spot once claimed by dry and barren ground. Its water was sky blue and rippling.

"Come," he repeated. "It'll do us good."

Musclebound Luigi, in a single motion, tore off all his clothes and bounded toward the water. Skin glistened. Muscles bulged. The hero again noticed how much larger and more defined the nude man was than himself. Biting his lip, he followed behind him, albeit walking instead of running. When he reached the lake, he remained fully clothed.

"Stop being silly," Musclebound Luigi said. "Get in before it all goes away, or changes to something else."

Musclebound Mario looked down at the water. "Is it cold?"

The man splashed around a bit. "No, it's great. Take off your clothes and dive in."

He dropped his overalls, exposing red bikini briefs with a cartoon head applied to the front.

"Cute," said Musclebound Luigi.

Embarrassed, the hero pulled up his overalls.

"No need to be ashamed. I'm not going to make fun."

He dropped them again. "Okay, but can I—can I keep my underwear on?"

"If you want."

"Thank you," he said and dove into the water.

Musclebound Luigi must have been more warm-blooded than he. Musclebound Mario jumped as if in shock when the water enveloped him. Shivering, feeling vulnerable, he swam out to the other man.

"Yes, my brother! Come!" Musclebound Luigi said as the hero approached him.

Side-by-side with his new friend, he felt too self-conscious to make eye contact. He tried to look down at his feet, but the water wasn't clear enough for him to see them, and he wondered if Bloopers and Cheep Cheeps were hiding below.

"You seem preoccupied," Muclebound Luigi said. "Just relax and let the water wash away your troubles."

He couldn't remember relaxing. He only remembered going through the motions of the same 32 stages in the same 8 worlds. But, after his unexpected trial, his muscles ached and his feet were sore, so Musclebound Mario closed his eyes, leaned his head back and allowed his body to simply float.

"There. Doesn't that feel good?"

He didn't hear this, for he'd already surrendered himself. Musclebound Luigi had been right. It was just what he needed, and it felt splendid, the water flowing past him, maybe through him. He sighed but was unaware that he'd done so.

Musclebound Luigi's voice brought him back to reality. "God," the man said, "you look awesome just floating there."

He looked up at him. "Really?"

"Yeah. Totally awesome." He reached over to squeeze Musclebound Mario's bicep. "So huge!"

The hero retracted his arm to conceal it behind his back. "But it's not as big as yours," he said.

"No worries, man. It's perfect just the way it is." His head titled slightly. He seemed to study the hero. "You believe that, don't you?"

Beneath the water, he twiddled his thumbs. "I suppose I do."

"Good. Never doubt it." He made a spinning motion with his index finger. "Now turn. Let me take a look at your back."

Musclebound Mario obeyed.

"Sweet," Musclebound Luigi said. "Tight ass lats, too. There are people who'd kill for those." He reached for Musclebound Mario's bicep again, his touch lingering this time. "Tell me, how much do you lift?"

"I don't know. A lot, I guess."

"I can lift 800,000 pounds."

Musclebound Mario spun to face the man. "Really? That's insane!"

"Perhaps we can challenge each other later. Would you like that? It'd be a friendly competition, and we could make a whole day of it."

"Maybe. But I really need to get back to my quest."

"Oh yeah." His brows scrunched. "What was that again?"

The suggestion that his quest was so minor it hadn't left an impression was borderline offensive. "A Prince," he said. "I've got to save him."

Musclebound Luigi flung up his hands, spraying water on Musclebound Mario. "Who cares about some crummy old prince? Princes can save themselves!"

"Wow, I said almost the same thing myself!"

"Isn't it crazy? I'm not sure we're two different people." Musclebound Luigi swam closer to him and stared without blinking into his eyes. After nearly a minute, he asked, "What did I just think?"

Musclebound Mario was clueless. He said, "That I'm, uh, a pretty cool dude?"

"Yes! That's exactly what I thought!"

"Are you fuckin' serious?"

"Totally fuckin' serious!"

Musclebound Mario gasped. Was this man his cosmic best-friend or platonic soulmate? He wanted to say something that expressed how he felt but words failed him. Perhaps such emotions were beyond words.

At that moment, Musclebound Luigi turned at the sound of crunching leaves and saw Musclebound Yoshi, who stood on the shore in bulky black swim trunks printed with white palm fronds and coconuts. A hole had been cut out to allow for his muscle-laden tail.

"Can I swim, too?" he asked, looking hopeful.

"No!" Musclebound Luigi screamed. "Go away!"

"Please! You said you'd let me next time, and next time is *this* time!"

The man reached down, dislodged a rock from the bottom of the lake and heaved it at Musclebound Yoshi's head. Yowling, the thing scurried off.

"Babbling idiot," said Musclebound Luigi. He turned back to the hero. "So, where were we again?"

"You were saying some really nice things to me."

"Oh yeah! And I'll keep saying them…but let's go farther out. We won't get interrupted, and there's this really interesting spot that I'm dying to show you."

They continued on. The lake seemed much larger when they

were deep inside of it. Before submerging himself, he could have sworn he'd glimpsed the opposite end. Now, all he saw was water extending to the horizon. He turned around but could no longer see the shore.

Still, they kept going. Musclebound Mario wanted to stop, ask questions, but figured the man had to know his way around the lake. Finally, Musclebound Luigi said, "Ah, here we are!"

The hero looked around. He saw nothing special. Just more water.

And the floating end of a rope.

Musclebound Luigi regarded the thing as it bobbed gently. "You know, this has always fascinated me."

"Really? It's just a rope."

"Yeah, but why is it here? Who placed it?"

"How should I know?"

"Where's your sense of curiosity, man? I've long wanted to pull it, but the time never felt right." He reached for the rope. "It feels right now that you're here."

Musclebound Mario tensed. "Maybe you shouldn't. It could be a trap."

"Come on, a little adventure won't hurt us!" He shot a sly glance. "Besides, you'd think a big, bad hero would have no fear of the unknown."

"Uh, I guess you're right."

"Of course I'm right." With a grin, he yanked the rope harder, and a huge pink cork bobbed to the surface. Air bubbles popped around it; the lake became a funnel. Musclebound Mario kicked and clawed, struggling against the swirl to find a grip. Musclebound Luigi hooted with joy until the lake emptied and into a drain he went. The hero followed him down, his body flapping and twirling and spinning—a slave to the pull of water.

He scraped against the walls of a narrow steel pipe and twisted through a bend that threatened to fold his legs over his stomach. Past the bend, there was light, first as a pinprick, then as a fast-approaching hole that seemed so very small. Musclebound Mario closed his eyes and felt not one impact, but two in rapid succession, and suddenly there was no more water.

He opened his eyes to a pixilated, side-scroll bathroom in which tinny music played without source. Across from him was an open toilet bowl, a Mario-head on the seat cover. He figured they must have shot through it before striking the ceiling and then the floor.

He regained his bearings and arose alongside Musclebound Luigi. Glancing down at his body and then at his friend's, he saw that they alone were not rendered in 8-bits.

Curiosity compelled him. He walked around the bathroom, looking down at the tub, which also had a Mario-head, and at the wallpaper, which featured thousands of heads, only tiny. Everything seemed at once familiar and foreign. "Where are we?" he asked.

"Watch out!" came Musclebound Luigi's reply.

There was the sound of simulated cannon fire, and a can of hairspray from the medicine cabinet flew at Musclebound Mario like a low-rent Bullet Bill.

He ducked, allowing the can to sail over his head and knock a hole in the bathroom wall. But the threat had not diminished. A trashcan flipped over and sprouted the head and legs of a Koopa Troopa. It adopted a slow yet deliberate crawl as long strips of toilet paper rose from the spilled debris and spun around in Firebar-mimicking circles.

Lousy, work-a-day objects had dared to pretend they were sacred things. Bile rose in Musclebound Mario's throat. Shouting, beating his chest, he rushed the trashcan and pounced atop it. The first strike crushed it, but he kept jumping, pulverizing the pieces that still clattered and clicked.

"Stop!" shouted Musclebound Luigi.

"No!" the hero shot back. "Let me enjoy this!"

"No time!" He pointed toward the medicine cabinet. "Look!"

Musclebound Mario turned. The cabinet glowed red as all things within it shook and came to life as a flurry of projectiles.

The two men jumped over the remains of the trashcan, contorted their bodies to dodge multiple bottles and cans midair. A somersault sent them over the tops of the toilet paper Firebars and into the bathroom door. It vanished in a puff of crudely rendered splinters.

Beyond, a short, empty hall led to a living room. In front of a TV with a picture of a friendly-looking Asian man atop it, stood an 8-bit, buzz-cut, body builder-type clad in red bikini briefs. Like the ones Musclebound Mario wore, there was a decal on the front, but the character was too small and lacked the detail for clarity.

The tiny villain flexed his muscles, jumped up and down and shook his fists with rage, but his programming was so basic that he appeared more sad than fearsome. He could not speak; the only sound he produced was the spring of his jump.

Musclebound Luigi laughed.

"Is that the boss?" said Musclebound Mario.

"I guess, but look at the guy. Aren't you glad you're nothing like him?"

"Yeah, man. Totally."

"So, should you stomp him first, or should I?"

The hero considered this as the villain continued to bounce in the same spot. "I might feel bad for doing that. I mean, he's no challenge at all."

The little man stopped at the sound of this, turned to the TV and, upon clasping his hands and kneeling, venerated the Asian man's image.

Stroboscopic flashes illuminated the room, and the boss began to grow—8-bit, 16-bit, 128-bit—lines and angles smoothing, features coalescing until he was a flesh-and-blood creature that cracked the ceiling. He glowered at the heroes with red, bloodshot eyes larger than their heads. The decal on the front of his briefs was visible now—an M, but curved to resemble a W.

The villain flung wide his arms, knocking down walls to reveal a hellscape of jagged rock and crimson flame. Booming brass, shrieking strings and crashing cymbals replaced the old soundtrack. The sound was stereophonic. Wagnerian.

Lips flared as the monster snarled and exhaled hot, angry breaths. "You are fucked," he said.

Musclebound Mario wished he had a shell like a Koopa Troopa. There, he could hide and think good thoughts until the threat wearied of him and left. But he was a hero and had a role to play.

Jumping in an attempt to flatten the Behemoth, he found that he could only reach the thing's naval. Up close, it looked like a cave or a black hole. He feared he might get sucked into it, but the boss swatted his head, sending him back to the floor and then up again. The boss began to dribble him.

Musclebound Luigi charged. The monster stopped toying with Musclebound Mario and flicked a big toe. Struck in the flank, the other man careened backwards through flames and into a stalagmite. He left an impression in stone when he pried himself from it to sprint back into battle.

"How the fuck do we defeat *that*!" Musclebound Mario screamed as he rolled from the path of a swooping, vein-swollen fist.

"I know of only one way!"

Relief buoyed him. Musclebound Luigi had a plan. "Great! How?"

His tone was solemn. "I must give freely of myself."

"Huh?"

The boss shot a wad of phlegm from his throat. It covered the men and forced them to scrape it from their faces before Musclebound Luigi could reply. "Just watch," he said. Raising and cocking both elbows, he aimed them at the boss.

Muscles tore loose and flew like so many bullets from Musclebound Luigi's arms. Musclebound Mario was amazed. It seemed as though the man had muscles-atop-muscles-atop-muscles.

The boss batted away the first and the second volleys. Biceps and radials, now useless, soared off into the flames and sizzled. The third, however, found its mark. His entire body quaked and he let out a brief roar.

Musclebound Mario turned back to his friend. Arms had grown progressively thinner, less muscularly defined. He imagined them reduced to flesh-wrapped bones and chilled. "No!" He seized the man's shoulder. "It's not worth it!"

Musclebound Luigi pulled away from him. "I already told you, it's the only way!"

Arms exhausted, he stood up straight and proud, arced his body and unleashed a storm of muscles from his legs and chest. Musclebound Mario could not bear to watch such sublime femorals, pecs and abdominals leave this man. Rather, he focused on the boss and was overjoyed to see him on the defensive.

So many projectiles, there was no way he could deflect them all. They struck him. Erased the hectoring smirk from his face. Eyes wide with fear, cringing and bleeding, he seemed pathetic. But Musclebound Luigi seemed a thing of majesty, his muscles departing his body like a swarm of butterflies to a sacrificial nest. Musclebound Mario felt shamed that his muscles were anchored to his bones. There, they looked good but did nothing.

The boss fell to his knees. A slender Musclebound Luigi turned his back to him and leaned over. "Now for the *coup de grace*," he said.

Perfectly formed glutes broke free from his ass. They grew as the boss had and continued to grow until they reached and were the size of the adversary. They framed him like bookends and smashed together. Rubbing one against the other, their friction worked to grind him down.

The boss shrieked until shrieks became moans and moans became silence. No longer did he have the bits required to empower speech, or even jump and produce a springy sound. Flicking, colors fading, he collapsed as the walls of the house reformed and the tinny music returned. Their work finished, the glutes fell together into a heap and liquefied.

The battle over, Musclebound Mario turned from the dying boss to congratulate, if not hug, Musclebound Luigi. But he found him on the ground, breathing hard and trembling. The hero ran over to him and saw his worst fears realized. The man was thinner than the actual Luigi. His cheeks were hollow, rheumy eyes rimmed in black. Further down, ribs and heart threatened to break through parchment skin. He was no longer beautiful. He was a sick old man.

"Oh fuck me!" said Musclebound Mario, not wanting to lose a new friend on the same day he'd found him. "Is there anything I can do?"

"Yes." He pointed a shaky, skeletal finger toward the boss. "Bring him...to me."

Musclebound Mario hurried over to the boss—a single, oversized pixel—picked him up and presented him to his wasted friend. "Here," he said. "Anything for you."

Musclebound Luigi forced a smile as he cradled the boss in his hand. "Not that big and scary now, are you?" he wheezed. Then he opened his mouth. Musclebound Mario turned away at the sight of yellow teeth and bloody gums, so he didn't see the man insert the villain and swallow him whole.

Immediately, thousands of tiny lightning bolts flickered across the length of his body, amassing to form a bright orb that enveloped him. In this incubator, cheeks reddened and fattened. Skin thickened and tautened. Muscles swelled and were reborn.

When the orb vanished, mere seconds later, Musclebound Luigi levitated from the floor and stood in mid-air, his arms open wide, a radiant smile on his face.

Musclebound Mario marveled. Though the man had become an ectomorph, his sacrifice had only heightened his good looks, softening areas that needed softening, deflating areas perhaps too swollen. He was streamlined yet buff. Elegant. The perfection of manhood. A statue atop a pedestal in a chamber fit for kings.

"Wow! Did you just Power Up?"

"Uh huh."

A large, blue button appeared on the wall beside them and blinked. Musclebound Luigi pressed it, and the room filled with water, water that was sucked back out by the reverse action of the toilet, returning them to the bowl and swirling them back down the pipes and out of them, back to the lake where they bobbed to the surface. Musclebound Mario thrashed in the water, gasping for air, but Musclebound Luigi, looking confident and composed, paddled effortlessly.

"Woo hoo, baby!" he said. "That was total blast!"

Musclebound Mario considered it more of a trial, but kept that sentiment to himself. "Sure was!" he said once he'd righted himself. Then, with less enthusiasm, he added, "But I wish I could have done *something* to help out."

"Nonsense. All you had to do was be there. Nothing bonds two men like defeating a shared enemy, you know."

Musclebound Mario sensed he was right, and that

warmed him over and above the water's chill. Had he finally found something to love and admire more than the One True Game?

"But I want to get even closer to you," Musclebound Luigi continued. "In fact, I won't be satisfied until there's no longer any separation between us, until we've melded mentally, physically and spiritually."

"Cool! I want that, too!"

The other man smiled widely, if not wisely. "Then it is settled. We must make a solemn vow to one another, and woe be unto he who breaks it!"

"Yeah! Woe be unto that dude!"

The man lifted his arms and spread them wide, as though to embrace the sky. "Repeat after me," he intoned.

Upon lifting his arms likewise, Musclebound Mario said, "Repeat after me."

Musclebound Luigi pursed his lips but continued, "I will always be your backup while on a quest."

"I will always be your backup while on a quest."

"If you lose a life, I will always be there."

"If you lose a life, I will always be there."

"Never will I forsake you."

"Never will I forsake you."

Musclebound Luigi bowed his head and opened his left hand. A golden ring appeared atop his palm. "Put this on your finger," he told Musclebound Mario.

The hero slid it onto his finger with great reverence, and a jubilant Musclebound Luigi exclaimed, "It is sealed, my brother! You're *my* mission, now and forever, and I wouldn't have it any other way!"

The hero had always wanted a questing partner, and this seemed so much better than having Bowser fill that role. Then and there, it no longer alarmed him that the world he once knew was falling apart. All that mattered was that Musclebound Luigi would never forsake him. "Fuck yeah, my brother! Fuck yeah!" he shouted, enraptured. "I am your mission, now and forever!"

Musclebound Luigi placed a calming hand on his shoulder. "Let's not get too worked up. Save it for later, when we're back home and the time is right."

"Home?" asked Musclebound Mario.

It seemed they had a hovel now. Dirt floor. Dry logs for walls. Wooden beams crisscrossed the ceiling below a thatched roof. The interior was tiny, but pane-less windows let in some light.

Inside, Musclebound Yoshi sat alone at a simple wooden table. He rested his head against the top, frowning. He appeared greener than usual.

Musclebound Luigi scowled at him. "Stop being lazy and clean this dump!"

"I can't," he moaned. "I feel sick."

"Oh really? What's wrong this time?"

"Berries. I ate them. But they looked so good!"

"Well, lard ass, you shouldn't eat everything you see."

"I wouldn't have eaten them if you'd have let me swim!"

"Don't you dare blame this on me!" He stalked up to Musclebound Yoshi and pointed toward the other side of the room. "Pick up that broom and get to work!"

"But I told—"

"Just do it!" Musclebound Luigi seized Musclebound Yoshi's seat and tilted it sharply to the left, spilling him onto the floor.

After picking himself up, the creature tried to heft a broom. Each time, it slipped from his awkward, stick-fingered grasp. Finally, he attempted to use his tongue, but swallowed the broom instead.

"Fuck it!" Musclebound Luigi snarled. "Do what you can without the broom!"

Musclebound Yoshi scurried about, scooping up trash and straightening things for a minute before his face blanched and he vomited in a corner. Musclebound Luigi appeared ready to unleash a tirade, but laughed instead when the creature slipped and fell into the mess.

Musclebound Luigi faced the hero. "Sorry," he said. "This is going to take a while, but we'll be together again later, and we'll be alone then. That I promise you."

Turning, Musclebound Mario saw a small door he hadn't noticed before. He walked to it. Opened it. The space behind it, empty except for a stool, was the size of a small closet.

As he closed the door, it sounded like Musclebound Luigi, with a groan, had hurled something heavy across the room. Musclebound Yoshi yelped as things broke.

The hero sat silently for a while, looking out at the world through a window. There, the afternoon passed him by, seeming long and uneventful but reassuring. It was nice to just sit around the Mushroom Kingdom for a change—what was left of it, anyway—watching objects rust, paint peel and ivy grow. It made time seem to slow like dripping molasses.

Without warning, a dried and dirty Koopa Troopa ghost wandered up to the window and paused to stare at him. "Find me," it said, voice like the wind.

Then a hand fell on Musclebound Mario's shoulder. He hadn't heard the door open and jumped a little before he realized it was only Musclebound Luigi. When he looked back toward the window, the ghost was gone.

"What are you thinking about?" the man asked him, smiling.

"Nothing really. I'm just sitting here."

"Well, Musclebound Yoshi is in his hole, and the place looks really good now, so I think we should both settle down for the night."

Musclebound Mario wondered where they might

sleep, but turned and saw that the room had expanded. Wedged into a corner, there was a straw-stuffed and moth-eaten mat.

"Only one?" he asked.

Musclebound Luigi shut the door, plunging the room into darkness. "One is all we need."

Musclebound Mario felt the other man's eyes upon him as he undressed. It was amazing, how much attention he offered. In the past, things came at him with vacant expressions in single-file lines. They had no love in their hearts. But this was very different, and very welcome.

Musclebound Luigi lost all his clothes but his underwear. His black boxer briefs had some big, dumb-looking guy's head applied to the front. Darkness blurred the details.

"Goodnight," the man said as Musclebound Mario got into bed beside him. "I love you."

"I love you, too," Musclebound Mario replied, and meant it.

When the hero closed his eyes, his mind tried to return to the worst things that had happened. So much fear and lack of confidence, it made him feel weak and unworthy of his physique. But then Musclebound Luigi curled up to him and began to spoon. The sensation of his new friend sharing warmth with him was comforting. Bad thoughts took flight, and he fell quickly to sleep.

Sunlight streamed in from a bay window and awoke Musclebound Mario from his slumber.

Overnight, the hovel had transformed into a quaint suburban-esque home. The wallpaper was a pastel floral print. A ceiling fan spun overhead as a central heater conditioned the air.

Musclebound Luigi had already gotten up. Musclebound Mario heard him tending to chores in another room.

But the hero didn't feel like arising yet. He luxuriated beneath the comforter and thought back on yesterday. Musclebound Luigi was such a cool guy, the best and single most awesome person to be his back-up man for this and every subsequent mission.

Finally, after almost an hour had passed, he arose. Hardwood flooring was cool against his feet. He gave himself a quick look-over in the dresser mirror before putting on his overalls and shirt.

He stepped out of the room to a hall, to a well-appointed living room and then to a kitchen that appeared stolen from a 50s-era suburban American home: Stove. Icemaker. Dishwasher. Linoleum. It hit all the right notes.

Musclebound Luigi stood at the stove. He wore an apron and scrambled eggs on the range top. Something else baked in the oven. The hero sniffed the air. Whatever was in the oven smelled delicious.

Musclebound Luigi turned at the sound of Musclebound Mario's footfalls. "Are you rested?" he asked him.

The hero stretched. "Sure am." He looked around. "Where's Musclebound Yoshi?"

"Off taking a shit or something. Who cares?" His lips formed a sudden smile. "Why don't you take a look behind you?"

Musclebound Mario turned. A trail of flowers had been spread out on the floor.

"Better see where those lead," said Musclebound Luigi.

Musclebound Mario followed the flowers to a cupboard across the room. There, on the middle shelf, sat a gaily-wrapped package.

"I bought you some new shoes!" He clasped a hand over his mouth. "Whoops! I gave away the surprise!"

Musclebound Mario brought the present with him

to a polished oak dinner table and opened it, expecting something old and hewn roughly from Goomba hide. Instead, there were expensive name brand shoes with tassels like little drumheads. Looking closely at it, he saw his reflection in shiny leather.

"Wow!" he effused. "These must have cost a fortune! Where did you find a place that sells shoes?"

"I know a guy. And I'll see about getting you a new pair of pants next time. Something tapered that shows off your backside."

Musclebound Mario sat at the table, and Musclebound Luigi came up behind him and tied a monogrammed bib to his neck. He then tied an identical one to his own.

Musclebound Yoshi entered the kitchen. Without looking at either man, he took a plate from the cabinet and filled it with food. As he passed, Musclebound Luigi extended his foot and tripped the creature. He fell to floor, face landing in his plate of biscuits and gravy.

"Don't mind him," Musclebound Luigi said. "That's the way he always eats."

Musclebound Mario burped. A full stomach was eminently satisfying. Hours had passed, however, and the amount of food on his plate never decreased. Having reached his limit, the hero hugged his bloated gut and said, "God, I feel fat! I need to burn this off immediately!"

"Tell me about it," said Musclebound Luigi. He removed the bib from his neck and tossed it atop the head of Musclebound Yoshi, who still ate on the floor.

"Too bad there's no place to work out around here."

"There isn't?" he said, slyly.

As if on cue, a kitchen wall retracted into the ceiling to reveal a full-scale gymnasium. Musclebound Mario heard the unmistakable clang of weights and barbells and the pulsing drone of techno music.

The other man nudged him. "Let's check this shit out."

"Hell yeah!"

Musclebound Luigi turned to Musclebound Yoshi, who tried to follow them. "This isn't for you, asshole!" he shouted.

They entered the gym. The floor was sliver and, while it provided traction, looked slick as ice. The walls were painted with orange and yellow lightning bolts over a bright blue background, and every piece of exercise equipment, down to the simplest dumbbells, appeared chrome-plated.

And there were no women here. Just men. Sweating. Heaving. Grunting. Huffing and puffing men.

Musclebound Mario's head darted this way and that. It was so unexpected, so difficult to process in its entirety, and the sound of clanking weights, stretching springs and pumping pedals was sheer intoxication. He felt the need to fling a man from a nearby Bow Flex and start using it, but restrained himself.

"This…is…*awesome*!" he said.

"Isn't it, though?"

They passed a reception desk, manned by a bald, silver-muscled robot with curly black chest hair. Musclebound Luigi waved at a group that waited there. "Hey Carlos. Hey John. Hey Roger. Hey Paul. Hey Philip," he said.

Musclebound Luigi seemed to know all the guys. "Where did these people come from?" Musclebound Mario asked him.

"Who knows? Who cares?" He grinned. "It's time to get ripped!"

The hero agreed, but, at that moment, realized he still wore the bib. Embarrassed, he tore it away and hoped no one had noticed.

Musclebound Mario, clad magically in a red tank top and gray workout shorts, lay supine on a bench, pushing up weights—450,000 pounds worth—connected to an iron bar.

Musclebound Mario didn't turn to see how many weights Musclebound Luigi was hefting. He feared the number might stagger him, if not sow the seeds of jealousy.

"Yeah, feel the burn!" said Musclebound Luigi.

The hero felt it. "This is the best day ever!" he said.

"Sure is," agreed Musclebound Luigi. "But tomorrow will be just as good, or better."

Indeed, he sensed it would be. And he sensed his body would only improve too, increasing in size until it filled and then exploded the room, the world and the universe. Then it would be an even more fitting temple to… to… He couldn't remember to what he had devoted himself.

Suddenly, a piece of paper fell from the ceiling and landed on the floor near Musclebound Mario's bench. He sat up to stare at it. "That's odd," he said. It wasn't simply paper, but a photograph of an Asian man.

Musclebound Luigi got up and walked over to it. His eyes widened. "No! Don't look at it!" He tried to kick it away, but Musclebound Mario's thoughts had already started to churn. Memories were dredged up. Light shone into dark places, and he remembered everything.

"My god! I've forgotten my mission!"

"What?"

"I can't pump iron! I've got to save the game!"

Musclebound Luigi gripped Musclebound Mario's shoulder. "No! Don't leave me!"

The gym floor quaked as a Piranha Pot shot through it, dislodging a set of free-weights. Bending its rubbery neck, it brought its mouth to the floor and opened it to the hero in invitation.

"You can't take him!" Musclebound Luigi shook a fist at the pot. "I won't let you!"

Musclebound Mario ran to it. The other man ran after him. Both jumped toward the mouth, yet Musclebound Luigi bounced from it as though he'd hit a force field.

The hero held onto the plant's lower lip, hands sinking into slimy, fatty flesh, so he wouldn't be sucked down immediately. "If you want in, get in!" he shouted. "But hurry!"

"I can't!"

"Yes, you can! Let it eat you!"

"That's what I'm trying to do!"

"Then what's the problem?"

Musclebound Luigi ground his teeth and pulled his hair. "I don't know! I just can't do it!"

Musclebound Mario surrendered to the pot's inner pull. "I'm sorry!" he screamed while going down, and was worlds away before his friend could voice a reply.

Then, upon being digested and reconstituted, he was disgorged into another realm.

PART FIVE:
THE OWNER

Suddenly, he was staring up at a cracked white ceiling, but not by choice. His neck wouldn't turn and his eyes wouldn't blink.

Then there were clomping footfalls, like those of a giant. He tried to arise, to flee, but found the rest of his body frozen, too. Seconds later, he was lofted into the air and saw that he was not in a house atop a beanstalk, but the living area of a seedy, probably three-room apartment.

His captor, flabby, balding and malodorous, was dressed in khaki shorts and a stained white t-shirt. He huffed as he walked and held Musclebound Mario in a clammy, mottled hand. The hero expected to be eaten, but the man moved him to a table on which an action-figure tableau, set in a dollhouse bedroom, had been constructed.

On the dresser, Lando Calrissian fucked Evil-Lynn, her legs spread so wide that, had she been human, bones would have snapped. On the floor, Han Solo did a line of coke off the back of Jem, the cartoon rock star, who was clad in black bondage gear, neck bent to appear broken. Above them, on the bed, Skeletor anally raped a Taun-Taun atop pink covers while strangling it with a garrote.

The man brought forth the action figure of a female medic and placed her beside Skeletor and the Taun-Taun. He fussed over the position of her arms and legs. Even fussed over the tiny sheets below. In time, his grimace became a yellow smile.

From the pocket of his shorts, he removed a model cock. It was long, thin and black. Veins like spider webs crossed its shaft. "This took ages to sculpt," he said, voice deep but breathy, like a heavy smoker. "Can't wait for everybody to see it in action."

The man rammed the cock into a hole that had been drilled into Musclebound Mario's featureless crotch all the way through to his ass. Then the man picked him up, laid him atop the medic so that his faux penis penetrated her faux vagina and positioned his hands around her neck.

"Perfect." The man licked his lips and rubbed his stomach. Beneath his shirt, fat rolls sometimes undulated, sometimes jiggled. "Just perfect."

But Musclebound Mario didn't feel as though it were perfect. He felt dehumanized. Sodomized. Violated.

The man snapped a quick picture of the scene with an expensive-looking camera before scurrying over to a computer. There, he plugged the camera into a dangling USB cable.

"How do you like that shit?" he said after a few minutes had passed. Musclebound Mario thought the man was talking to him before realizing he had engaged another deviant online.

"I love the new dick! And the look on Skeletor's face is priceless!" said the other deviant. "It's like he's just becoming aware that he's hate-fucking a Taun-Taun, and is like, *what the shit?*"

"Thanks, man. I've been really creative lately, and this new dick is going to take me to the next level."

"You should make posters or something. I'd buy one, especially if you use that cool new figure. What was it again?"

"Musclebound Mario," the man said. "He's a one-of-a-kind toy. You don't want to know the things I had to do to get him. Nasty things. Terrible things."

"And I'd bet you'd do them all again!"

"Hell, yeah! I'd do 'em in a heartbeat!" The man turned back to his frozen menagerie. "But I just wanted your opinion. Gotta rearrange the set for the next shoot."

He pulled Musclebound Mario free from the medic and placed him atop Jem where he snorted coke as Cobra Commander and Snake Eyes gang raped a Go-Bot in the open closet. A minute later, the hero held a knife to She-Ra's throat, his cock penetrating not only her ass, but protruding two inches through the hole in her crotch. Optimus Prime knelt before them both and sucked the head.

And then he was fucking soldier figures, policemen figures, fantasy figures, animal figures—on and on and on as days piled into weeks and months, his plastic crotch pounding against so many other plastic vaginas, mouths and asses that all holes became one big hole that threatened to swallow him.

Often, Musclebound Mario caught glimpses of the other action figures doing drugs or sucking a dick or eating out a pussy and felt that they were all ghosts, forever replaying the same scenes of drunken and hedonistic debauchery, unaware that they could never break free from the cycle, or even that they were trapped at all. It was like a Bosch painting. Like Hell.

One day, he was taken into the Owner's bedroom for a private session.

"I know you need to be in pictures," he said to Musclebound Mario, his expression quite grave, "but there'll be no cameras here, and everything we do can never leave this room."

The Owner tossed him to the bed. "You'll have no dignity when I'm through with you."

Musclebound Mario was certain his dignity had been erased long ago.

Fingers pulled roughly at his legs, almost snapping the rubber bands within. "Spread 'em wide, motherfucker!" the Owner snarled.

Musclebound Mario wanted to yell, 'stop!' or, baring that, think-scream so forcefully that the man had to hear him, but neither things happened.

The Owner stared at him. "In a compromising position, I see."

The hero wondered if the man could sense his fear.

"No longer so confident, are you, Tim?"

Tim?

"You've finally figured out who's in charge." The Owner twisted Musclebound Mario's left arm until it nearly popped out of joint. His expression became one of uncorked rage. "You fucked up my life in school!" he screamed. "You had to be so hot and muscular! So rugged and handsome! Well, no more glory days for you, Mr. Perfect! You could have any girl you want, but you're not going to have one today! No, sir!" He unbuttoned his pants and whipped out his thick, stubby cock. "You're going to take it from *me!*"

The Owner worked the shaft. "You're a little slut, aren't you?" he repeated, over and over again until Musclebound Mario believed it.

Yes, the hero thought. *I'm a little slut.*

"I can take anything I want from you."

You can take anything you want from me.

"I can make you my little bitch."

You can make me your little bitch.

The man jacked it harder, faster. His penis, a grower-not-a-shower, extended farther than Musclebound Mario had thought possible. Though the Owner stood feet from him, the head was flush with his plastic face. "Fuckin' shit, yeah!" he moaned. "Fuckin' shit, yeah! It's a comin'!"

The Owner shot semen all over him. His plastic body somehow felt the hot, sticky spray. "Suck my spunk, you asshole!" the man shrieked.

But he couldn't suck it. He could only remain on the bed, blank-faced and immobile.

This fact angered the Owner. With a bestial groan, he picked up and threw Musclebound Mario's figure against the nearest wall before storming back into the living room.

Years seemed to pass, and it began to seem less like Hell and more like Purgatory. Musclebound Mario had almost grown accustomed to the daily simulations of sodomy. He thought, maybe, that it would be tolerable if only he were getting paid. They were, after all, just plastic. Toys that served no other purpose than to fuck and be fucked. Vaguely, it seemed that there had once been more to life. At one time, he'd been on a quest.

What quest was that again?

Try as he might, he couldn't answer the question.

Existence had become hollow and meaningless.

Then the Owner made a new purchase: a female fighter pilot action figure.

He didn't know her name, or, rather, what her figure was called, so he dubbed her Ezmerelda. Perhaps her figure was modeled after someone of Portuguese descent. Her face was long and slender, her skin a bit olive like his own. Lips were ruby red. Saucer-shaped eyes were brown.

Though he fucked her like the others, he nevertheless felt that she was special. "Please, forgive me," he'd wanted to say when he saw what he imagined to be pain and anguish in her plastic eyes, but his mouth was painted on, and he had no vocal cords.

During more lucid moments, he wondered if he was fooling himself and his was the only figure with a soul.

But that was before *her* figure winked at him and her lips puckered to blow a kiss *his* soul caught.

It wasn't a trick of light and shadow. At that instant, he knew that she had been there all along, that she loved him as he loved her and that he would always be with her, no matter what trials and tribulations came.

He felt her aura then. So vital, it penetrated him and throbbed in his veins, stronger than the pulse of blood. Gazing into her eyes, he imagined their life together. When they fucked, it would be on their own free will, and it would be an act of beauty. Then he imagined the kids they would have—wonderful, plastic children that never got into trouble or ate or aged.

Theirs would be a perfect life.

At some point, the Owner, his camera in hand, scooped Ezmerelda up and took her outside. This worried Musclebound Mario. Never before had an action figure left the apartment.

Minutes later, he heard a *bang*, and the man reentered the room. He positioned Musclebound Mario's figure so that it faced the computer, took his customary seat and, to the fellow deviant, said, "I just did the fucking coolest thing ever!"

"Shit yeah, man! Can't wait to see it!"

The owner pushed a button; a media player opened on the screen. "It's totally intense."

"Cool! Send it over!"

"Nope. The first viewing is always private. You should know that by now."

"Come on. I won't—"

He shook his head. "Sorry. I'm selfish in that way."

"Wait—"

"I'll call you back soon."

The chat-session over, the Owner turned to

Musclebound Mario. He had a smug, self-satisfied look on an acne-scarred face.

When the man spun back around, Musclebound Mario watched him view a video of Ezmerelda being blown apart. Through the hole that went from her crotch to ass, the Owner had inserted a firecracker and lit the fuse.

"Shit! Oh shit! That was so awesome!" he screamed on video.

The words would have broken Musclebound Mario's heart, were it there to break.

The man rewound the video. Watched it again.

The loss Musclebound Mario felt was incalculable. He fell into a stupor, a funk. He went through the motions of each new photo shoot, feeling nothing, thinking nothing. He was a mindless, soulless whore, and that was all he deserved to be. So jaded, he hadn't realized that his figure had fallen behind a box and had been lost to the Owner until a layer of dust covered it.

At some point—time was meaningless—a solider figure he'd once sodomized fell behind Musclebound Mario's box. It landed atop him with a painless *click*. The soldier's face was pressed against his face, and he had to look into it for so long that it ceased to be a face at all.

Perhaps a billion years later, the Owner knocked Musclebound Mario's figure over the edge of the shelf when he moved the box that concealed it. The soldier figure— Musclebound Mario had completely forgotten about it prior to that moment—fell, too.

Rather than hitting shag carpeting, he found himself in a moist and muscular tunnel that seemed familiar, the soldier figure turning and tumbling alongside him.

PART SIX:
RETURN OF THE MUSCLEBOUND

The pot spat him into a Mushroom Kingdom so hot he could feel, taste and see the heat.

The entire world had become a pixilated desert. Nothing living stood atop its sands. No plants grew. No villains wandered. There were only crumbling Goomba skulls and fading Koopa Troopa shells.

Musclebound Mario felt like he'd been born again into this world, and that he'd have to relearn the most basic functions of life, so he remained on the sand, staring up at the sunless yet somehow bright sky.

At some point, minutes or hours later, he remembered a name: *Musclebound Luigi*. It took him a few minutes more to recall his own.

An inner fog seemed to lift. He felt his strength return and prepared to arise. Turning, he saw two dead eyes that stared sightlessly back at him. The hero gasped then recoiled. A male corpse in a military uniform lie there, face pale and moon-like in death.

Jumping up, he looked around for Musclebound Luigi. In the distance, he spotted him. Hunched on the ground, the man appeared as a dot against the stark and unforgiving landscape.

Musclebound Mario walked on legs that wobbled. The sand baked his feet as the air cooked his back. He wanted to get to his friend as soon as possible. He defied his unsteady legs and began to run.

"Finally up, are you?" said Musclebound Luigi when he reached him.

The hero was elated. He wanted to embrace the man so tightly that it might deflate both their muscles, but Musclebound Luigi continued to sit there, hands squeezing something above a crude wooden cup. When he turned, he held the cup and stared at it instead of Musclebound Mario. "Want water?" he said, no emotion in his voice.

"Yes, please."

He handed him the cup. "Don't drink it all, okay."

Seemed like an odd request. Still, the hero accepted the cup with a hand that shook. The cup slipped from his grasp. The thirsty sand drank up the water in an instant.

Musclebound Luigi, face set in a tight scowl, growled, "Be careful with that!"

"It's just water, man."

"Just water, eh? I'll have you know it's the first water I've had in years!"

"Years?"

"Yes, *years*!" He unclenched his other hand, revealing a rock. "I sit here and wring stones until I have a full glass. Do you have any idea how long that takes?"

"No, I—"

"And, once I've got all the water I can get, I gather more stones and wring them, again and again and again!"

"You really…wring stones?"

"Yes!"

"But what about the house? The gym?"

He threw up his hands. "Gone! Gone for so long they might as well never have existed!"

"How long was *I* gone?"

"Oh, I don't know. About a hundred thousand *forevers*!"

Musclebound Mario was at a loss, so he decided to tell him about the corpse.

The other man got up and walked toward the pot.

"What are we going to do?" Musclebound Mario asked when they reached the body.

"Throw it back. It doesn't belong here."

He shivered at the thought of touching dead flesh.

"Hell, I'll do it!" The man pushed Musclebound Mario aside. "It's not like you've been here to do much of anything lately." Picking up the corpse, he tossed it into the mouth of the pot like so much garbage.

Musclebound Mario wandered behind Musclebound Luigi, wanting to follow him back to the cup and the rocks he squeezed, wanting to talk with him and find out why he seemed so cold and distant.

When they stopped, the rocks and cup were gone. Musclebound Luigi stared at the sand as though doing so might make them reappear.

"You feeling okay?" Musclebound Mario asked him.

"About as fine as can be expected, no thanks to you."

Musclebound Mario pursed his lips before saying, "You're being awfully short with me."

"At least I'm not Mr. Neglectful."

"What?"

He shrugged. "Oh, you know. You get spat out, and what's the first thing you do?" He raised a fist. "You lie there for hours!"

Did Musclebound Luigi not understand that he'd just undergone a trial? "It wasn't paradise for me, either!" he exclaimed.

"Oh, so it's all about you?" He harrumphed. "Typical."

The hero experienced an emotion he never imagined he'd feel toward his friend: utter frustration. "Look," he said.

"I don't want to start shit. I hardly know you, but I think you're a cool guy and—"

"Sorry," Musclebound Luigi interjected, "but you've already started shit."

"Relax, brother. You—"

Teeth clenched like fists. "Brother? *Brother*! How dare you call me that! You really are an inconsiderate ass, aren't you?"

"I'm not the ass!" Musclebound Mario huffed. "You were so cool at first. What's gotten into you, man? What's your problem?"

"What's gotten into *me*? What's *my* problem? My problem is *your* problem!"

"I don't get you. Why—"

Neck veins bulged as he began to shout. "If you think anybody wants you like I do, you're mistaken! You're my quest! Take you away and there's nothing left for me but that Musclebound Yoshi asshole!" His eyes narrowed. "And you left me with him!"

Musclebound Mario was incredulous. "You couldn't go through the pot!"

"You could have *made* me go! You're Musclebound Mario!"

He opened his mouth to speak.

"No! I don't want to hear it! I know what's best for you and how to attend to your needs! Yet how do you repay me?"

"I—"

"Zip it! You repaid me by breaking your vow!"

"My vow?"

He cocked his head. Looked askance at him. "You don't remember?"

"No, I—"

He stepped a little closer. "Seriously?"

Musclebound Mario felt trapped. "I wish I did! I want to! But—"

"You said you would always be with me, on every quest! You said you would have my back, always! But you did none of that, ever!" Musclebound Luigi glanced down at Musclebound Mario's hand. "And where's the ring?"

"Ring?"

"You've forgotten about that, too!"

"Oh yeah. I guess it fell off."

"*You guess it fell off.*" The man's entire body quaked. "*You ass-fucking cock sucker!*"

"Hey now, you'd better—"

"You're no hero! You're a nobody—a big, fat fuck—and your muscles are shit compared to mine!"

Musclebound Mario could not listen to this. He shouted, "And you're a total asshole!" though, deep inside, he feared the man had spoken the truth about his muscles.

Musclebound Luigi shrugged. "Takes one to know one."

"If you're going to be like this, then I'm out!" With that, the hero stormed away, kicking sand and cursing.

Musclebound Mario wandered aimlessly. He had no way of knowing how long or how far he'd traveled, or if he had gone in circles. Even now, he had a hard time believing his friend hadn't pranked him.

But what if the truth was worse? Living in such a stark environment for so long couldn't have been good for him. What if he'd contracted some disease?

Musclebound Mario didn't want to consider this, so he focused on the barren landscape. It still resembled a desert, but the few things in it had become harder to focus on, less contrastable. He approached a cardboard castle, missing its top half and streaked with black ichors. Semi-transparent, it seemed flicker in and out of existence like quicksilver. He reached out, and his hand traveled through it.

He didn't want to think about this, either, so he

blanked his mind and shut his eyelids. He kept them closed as he walked. When finally he opened them, he saw Musclebound Yoshi sitting listlessly on a sand mound, likewise self-sequestered, likewise moping.

Musclebound Mario felt he had to talk to someone, and—damn it—Musclebound Yoshi was the only available option. The hero took an uncomfortable seat beside the creature. "Hey," he said after almost a minute had passed.

"Why are you taking to me?" Musclebound Yoshi turned his gaze to the ground. "You don't want to talk. You want to be mean."

"What the hell? I'm not trying to be mean."

"You think ganging up on me is a good thing, then?"

"I'm sorry, okay. Guess I didn't realize what I was doing at the time."

"I don't think you realize what you're doing now."

Musclebound Mario groaned. "If you're going to be like this, then I don't have to talk to you, either!"

When the hero made to rise, Musclebound Yoshi flailed his tiny arms and said, "No, don't leave! I'm so lonely it doesn't matter what you say or do to me!"

The hero sat back down. "You're all messed up, aren't you? What's your deal, anyway?"

"Can't you figure it out?" Musclebound Yoshi's tone hardened. "I was so happy to see you yesterday. A friend was just what I needed." His face scrunched. "But then you turned into another asshole and destroyed my chances of ever again having hope!"

Musclebound Mario hadn't realized this creature was so despondent. "I told you I was sorry earlier," he said. "Now, I mean it."

"Really? You do?"

"Yes, I do."

The creature contemplated this for a while. "Okay,

I'll accept your apology—for now." Then he sighed. "Go ahead. Say what you have to say."

The hero lowered his voice, though he knew it was silly. The world felt so empty that Musclebound Yoshi seemed like the only other living thing. He said, "What the fuck's up with Musclebound Luigi?"

Musclebound Yoshi's entire upper body moved as he shrugged. "Dunno. He's always been that way."

"That can't be right. He was so cool before. The best guy ever."

"Cool to you, maybe, but never to me."

"Why stick around him, then?"

"Because I don't want to be alone. Why else?"

"Can't you find a better friend?"

"What the hell kind of question is that?" He gestured rapidly in all four directions. "I haven't seen anyone but him or you…ever!"

"Okay, sure. You have a point. But what does he do to you that's so bad?"

"Everything."

Musclebound Mario arched his brows. "Do you deserve it?"

"No!"

"Then why does he do it?"

The creature paused for a bit and said, "I'll tell you if you promise not to laugh."

"I won't laugh."

"But do you mean it? Do you *promise*?"

"Yes, I promise."

Musclebound Yoshi fidgeted as though overcome with ants. "Maybe… I don't know…"

"I already promised, man! Now spill it!"

"I'm… How to say it?" Twiddling his fingers, he said, "I'm not, uh, what people think I am."

Musclebound Mario stared vacantly at him.

"I'm not…entirely male."

"You're gay?"

"No!" he shouted, suddenly flustered. "I'm a hermaphrodite, and that's why Musclebound Luigi hates me! He tells me that I'm stupid and a freak, okay! Is that what you want to hear?"

The hero was stunned into silence. Then, "Uh, okay. Should I, uh, call you 'he' or 'she?'"

Again, the thing sighed. "Stick with 'he.' I'm used to it."

"Okay, but…but really…you're a *hermaphro-fuckindite*?"

Musclebound Yoshi paled. "I thought you were cool with it!"

"Sure, but does that mean you can, you know, make babies with yourself?"

"Yes, yes! Stop rubbing it in!" He bowed his head. His tone dropped an octave. "I shouldn't have told you, because now you hate me, too!" Sobbing, Musclebound Yoshi tried to blow his nose into his palm, but his arm was too small to reach it. "Damn my body!" he shouted.

Musclebound Mario felt chastised. He had to make amends. Reaching out, he hugged Musclebound Yoshi tight. Pressed up against him, the creature seemed less like a lizard and more like a kid. "Everything will be okay," he said. "I promise."

Musclebound Yoshi looked up at him, eyes red, wet and pleading. "So, you'll stop him from beating me, too?"

"He *beats* you?"

"All the time! And he puts his fingers in my holes when I'm trying to sleep."

"Holes? Which ones?"

Eyes swelled. "*All of them*!"

"My god, what a total fucker!"

"Please don't tell him I said any of this!" Musclebound

Yoshi did his best to clasp his hands in a prayer position. "Don't! Please!"

Righteous power flowed from Musclebound Mario's heart into his fists. He felt more electric than when he had absorbed Fire Flowers. "Oh, I'll do better than tell him. And I'm sorry I ever misjudged you, friend. You're a good guy, or girl...whatever. I can't believe Musclebound Luigi is such a bastard, and I can't believe I ever admired—"

All at once, a ring of sand in front of them collapsed into a crater and erupted, raining rocks and fragments of bone on both hero and hermaphrodite. When the debris cleared, Musclebound Luigi held a squirming Musclebound Yoshi aloft by the neck. "I expected you'd find and talk with this son of a bitch," he said, "and I was right."

"Put him down!" Musclebound Mario demanded.

"Whatever you say." Musclebound Luigi squeezed Musclebound Yoshi's neck. The creature's eyes popped from their sockets. Limbs spasmed as blood, urine and fecal matter spilled onto sand. Upon releasing his grip, a limp body crumpled at the man's feet.

Musclebound Mario ran to it, cradled its head in his hand, but resurrection of the dead was beyond the scope of his powers.

"Why bother?" Musclebound Luigi scoffed. "He wasn't part of the one thing you love."

The desire to kill this man burned within the hero. Instead, he looked up and said, "Just walk away. As much as I might want, I cannot harm a Luigi."

The man's smile was a razor. "I never told you what I am."

Musclebound Mario glared. "What are you, then?"

"I was going to tell you later—in the dark, perhaps— but let's get it done with now." Musclebound Luigi tugged beneath his shirt collar, revealing the bottom flap of a latex mask. He lifted the mask from his face and unzipped a body suit. From it, a scrawny middle-aged man with thinning hair and crooked teeth emerged. "I win the Best Costume award every year," he said.

Betrayal caused something within the hero to break. "You're a monster like those others!" he shouted.

The Conventioneer grimaced. "You think this doesn't hurt me? And fuck those others! They wanted 8x10s and figurines. They didn't care for the man. When they wanted to eat you, I wanted to *know* you!" He took a few aggressive steps toward Musclebound Mario. "Hell, I even wanted to love you and be with you forever! And we could have had everything and more, but you had to get curious, didn't you? You had to fuck things up!"

Musclebound Mario adopted a combat stance. Rather than attack, the Conventioneer hurtled insults. "You're a little bitch. You know that, right?"

A part of him wanted to sulk, though he couldn't in good conscience allow himself that when Musclebound Yoshi lay dead.

"You'd better know, 'cause it's the truth."

To prove him wrong, Musclebound Mario socked him in the stomach. Wincing, clutching his gut, the Conventioneer squeaked out, "You're a wimp, and a child could kick your lame ass."

When Musclebound Mario tried to punch him in the mouth, his swing went wild.

"And your muscles are tiny."

Through the corner of his eyes, he saw both his arms begin to shrink. The sleeves of his shirt, once tight against his skin, flapped in a slight breeze. He ran up to his attacker before he could reduce him further and struck him in the lips. The force generated failed to move the man's head.

"Not tiny," he gloated. "Non-existent."

His legs folded beneath him, no longer powerful enough to support even his rapidly diminishing weight.

"Yeah, that's right. You're just a speck on the ground."

That didn't seem far from the truth as Musclebound Mario wallowed and squirmed atop a pile of grossly oversized clothing. He tried to say something to the Conventioneer, who circled him while grinning, but his voice was not unlike the muffled chirp of an insect.

The Conventioneer leaned over to stroke the hero's cheek with a cold, dead hand. It said, "Looks like you're ready to see the real me."

Blackening and swelling, its body burst free from its clothing. Limbs lengthened and bent at odd angles. Eyes segmented, and a third opened not on its forehead, but on a thin, orange-green tongue that swung from the cave opening of its mouth. Hot, stinking salvia dripped from stalactite teeth and scoured the hero's face as its fingers stretched and twisted through the air. They bound Musclebound Mario's arms and legs and coiled about his belly and back—an organic, full-body restraining device.

The Conventioneer licked its spit off his cheek. "You taste so good," it said.

Musclebound Mario could only wince.

Teeth grew past the monster's chin. Tips auto-filled into razors. "Maybe I should just eat—"

Behind them: a hacking sound. A bolus shot up a Piranha Plant's throat. The plant heaved, and, in the moments that followed, expelled the Owner into the remains of the Mushroom Kingdom. Stuffed in his pants was the fake penis, now the size of a pole. Behind him, he dragged the corpse of a brown-haired, olive-skinned woman dressed as a fighter pilot.

Musclebound Mario remembered Ezmerelda. Though the Owner had apparently bought a new figure— one, perhaps, without a soul—he still felt the pang of loss.

97

The Owner faced him. "So, there you are! I've been looking all over for you!"

The Conventioneer sneered at the new arrival. "Get your ass back in that pot! You don't deserve him!"

"The hell I don't!" The Owner pulled a slip of paper from his pocket. "I've got the receipt!"

The Conventioneer retracted its fingers, picked up Musclebound Mario's wasted body and clamped it to its chest. "You never loved him, so you'll never get to keep him!"

Nonchalant in the face of horror, the Owner stalked up to the thing and, upon leashing an extended, sulfurous fart, said, "It's not about love. It's about *use*."

The Conventioneer clutched Musclebound Mario tighter as the Owner grabbed hold of the hero and began to tug.

"I had him the longest!" shouted the Owner.

"I saw him fir—"

The Owner obliterated its words with a slug to the face. Musclebound Mario, amazed that the man, so fat and globular, could hold his own against a total fucking monster, was taken down with the creature. It tried repeatedly to stand. Each time, the Owner slapped it down with the prop penis. Grunting and farting with exertion, perhaps his power and vitality sprang from sheer repulsiveness.

Finally, the Conventioneer dodged a slap. Rolling to its feet, it elongated its fingers and enveloped them around the Owner as it'd done with Musclebound Mario. They slid against and crisscrossed the man's body and wormed into every hole and orifice.

"Oh yeah, that's nice," the Owner said, words muffled due to the fingers prying past his lips. "But more ass-play, please." With a sudden heave, he broke through the maze as though fingers were twigs.

"Fuck, that hurts!" said the Conventioneer.

The Owner rubbed his eyes and feigned tears. "Aw, I'm so sorry. Want a band aid, you big, fat pussy?"

Fists clenched, nostrils flaring, the Conventioneer pursed its lips and spat a thick and corrosive glob of green slime at the Owner. The man caught it in his left hand, screamed as his flesh sizzled, yet took that same hand and shoved it hard into the monster's face.

It staggered blindly, howling, until the Owner tackled it and sent both their bodies to the ground. The Owner straddled the Conventioneer. Like an overturned beetle, it flailed its arms and legs uselessly.

The hero, likewise on his back, couldn't make himself care if man or beast won.

The Owner spun the Conventioneer around so that it faced him. Hefting the phallus, he centered it over a scaly chest and, with a shout of ecstasy, drove it in deep. Purple blood spewed from the Conventioneer's nose and mouth. Claws slid to its sides. It went limp as segmented eyes closed and a hideous tongue lolled from a steaming but soon to cool maw.

The Owner regarded the thing. "Looks like I got it good. Too bad the dick isn't in the right place, though." He wrenched the dick free, turned to the helpless hero and twisted out a smile. "I won't make that mistake again."

Musclebound Mario watched the man approach the female corpse. Picking it up, he dragged it to Musclebound Mario and dropped it inches from him. The hero could not bear to look into the fighter pilot's unblinking eyes, but was too weak to turn away.

"I bought a new figure because I could tell you had a thing for the old bitch." The Owner paused to soak in her form. "God, I *really* like how toys are in this world. Don't you?"

Musclebound Mario said nothing.

Now, the Owner loomed over him. "Too bad you're all skinny and stupid looking, but whatever." The man stroked and admired the black shaft, seemingly lost in its branching network of veins. "The cock's the real star of the show."

Musclebound Mario opened his mouth. Something like words emerged.

The Owner lifted a hand to an ear. "Did you say something?"

He managed to eek out, "I—I just want to…play game…now…please."

The Owner snorted. "Save your breath. It doesn't matter what you want." At that moment, something like fire erupted in his eyes. "As your master, I alone matter, and now I command you to fuck this dead bitch!" He raised the faux dick high, aiming it over Musclebound Mario's crotch. The hero saw the dirt and blood that adhered to it and felt insane worrying about cleanliness when its sharp tip seemed destined to pierce his scrotum.

There was a moan. The Owner turned to the Conventioneer. Meekly, it crawled toward him, one claw raised and trembling as it kneaded air.

"You—won't—take—him," it wheezed.

The Owner inhaled. Exhaled. Lowered the dick. "Excuse me for a second," he said.

Behind him, the hero heard a howl that dissolved into a gag. Then there was a wet, sloshy sound, like the Owner was sawing through the monster's throat, perhaps with its own fingernails. Finally, there was silence, and, in that instant, Musclebound Mario's muscles re-inflated like balloons. They had only been gone for minutes, but oh how he'd missed them.

Still, he lay quietly on the ground.

The Owner returned to him. "There, now. Looks like we're—" He saw fat biceps and obscenely swollen lats. His mouth became an O.

Musclebound Mario jumped up, grabbed the faux phallus and spun counterclockwise until he stood behind the Owner.

The Owner sputtered like he had something to

say. Musclebound Mario didn't give him time for that. He throttled him with the ruined dick.

The Owner's face went from peach to red to purple. He first spat saliva then blood as his body pounded against Musclebound Mario's. It was so up close, so personal. The hero was surprised, and then ashamed, to find that he'd become aroused.

"Come on, you fucker!" he shouted. "Die for me! Please!"

The Owner's eyelids fluttered. He tremored a final time and went momentarily rigid. Finally, body sagging, the man gave up both the fight and the ghost.

Musclebound Mario leaned over him, looked into his eyes and checked his pulse. Only then was he satisfied.

Musclebound Mario wanted to lean against something—the act of murder had drained him—but there was nothing to lean against, so he spent a few moments standing there, coming to terms with himself and his act. Then he did what he knew had to be done.

The hero walked up to the female corpse, took it beneath its arms and dragged it across the sand back to the pot.

Slowly, mournfully, the pot lowered itself so that its bottom lip met the ground. Musclebound Mario paused briefly at that humid, sticky maw, then, very gently, lifted the corpse and slid it inside the mouth so it could reenter its intended realm and be a toy again.

Finally, he allowed himself to sit on sands that were slowly draining of color, becoming like shrinking salt crystals. It seemed that there was nothing beneath the sand, and no separation between earth and sky. And it dawned on him that he could no longer feel heat.

PART SEVEN:
TO THE CASTLE AND BEYOND

Musclebound Mario, face cradled in his hands, sat in the same spot long after the world had been reduced to a white void. Had he failed, he wondered? Was killing the Owner not enough?

Maybe he had always been an unworthy hero.

Sighing, he looked up. Rather than emptiness, he beheld a mountain atop which a castle, like a tall, leering vulture of black spires and turrets, was perched. Neither decayed nor pixilated, it was the one thing in the world that seemed real.

Hope restored, he arose, stretched his muscles and prepared to begin the trek.

Hours passed. The castle and its mountain were no closer than before. He tried to run and execute multiple expansive jumps, but there was no traction to be found in nothingness.

He imagined himself walking in place forever. Growing old. Bones crumbling. Muscles withering. Nearing defeat, his mind returned to the things he missed most. Flagpoles and staircases built of blocks. Dark but predictable caves and bridges and pulleys that hung without anchor in the sky. If only he could see them again!

It was then he noticed that a dark shadow on the front of the mountain was really the gaping mouth of a cave.

He imagined the things that might be inside it and purged all troubling thought. He wouldn't give up. He would keep walking; die walking, even. It didn't matter if he never reached the goal. He would play Sisyphus and do so with a happy heart.

Sometime—whenever—something long, thin and green proceeded from the cave's mouth. Quickly yet silently, it floated toward him. Musclebound Mario bristled at the sight, but relaxed when he recognized the object as a Piranha Plant Pot, turned on its side.

Darkness overtook him as the pot drew him in. Muscles pushed down hard against his body, speeding him up until he was shot, full-blast, out the opposite end of the pot. The skin on his face peeled back. His shirt and overalls were torn away. Tightly, he clung to his briefs, not wanting to fight the enemy-of-enemies completely nude.

Head-over-heels, he flew past the mouth of the cave before skidding to a halt against a phallic stalagmite. There, for the first time, he saw his blood. He marveled at how red it was before he arose and dusted himself off.

Twirling Firebars on the ground and ceiling lit a path. Musclebound Mario was relieved to find something so familiar. It provided a sense of warmth. Perhaps he'd even happen upon a mushroom or a cache of coins.

But there were no mushrooms. No coins. Just utter darkness as, suddenly, the torches were snuffed out.

And then there were voices.

"You'll never make it."

"You'll die.

"Give up."

Those voices were serpentine, seductive. Musclebound Mario slammed his hands over his ears, but felt invisible fingers run nails across his back, tickle his neck and stroke his chest, eliciting sensations that weighed down his body, mind and soul.

And, now, he heard the voices inside his head, too.

"Stay with us," they said.

"Go no further."

"It's safe here."

"So safe..."

He shook his head. Dislodging voices. Moving forward into darkness. Arms extended and hands groping, he placed total confidence in his internal radar.

Following an abrupt turn, the trail ended. Before him: the entryway into a huge circular chamber. Stalactites hung from the ceiling. Fat mushrooms and green, bioluminescent moss sprouted on a floor that appeared hand-hewn.

Musclebound Mario entered the room and there beheld walls adorned with Koopa Troopas, their shells sliced off and replaced backwards, or draped over their heads like oversized hats. On the floor, a Goomba on a rack was drawn out to twelve times its intended length. Another Koopa Troopa, collapsed in a corner, was a neglected, chain-draped skeleton.

The thing lifted its head, dust drifting from its bones. "Help me," it said to him.

The hero turned away quickly. Gooseflesh prickled his skin. What a foul chamber. It felt like a graveyard where corpses never slept and were tormented.

Above him, he heard a mechanized rumble. It was the sound of a thin, white screen descending from the ceiling. Once it had locked into position, a stream of bright projector light shone from a hidden booth, and a movie of sorts began.

He saw Luigi. His eight-bit body had been hacked to tiny pieces. Still, the pieces flopped as though attempting an improbable escape. Musclebound Mario knew who this was, or had been, because he recognized half a moustache on a vivisected hunk of flesh.

He saw Mario, stripped down to his eight-bit tighty

whities and tied to a chair. A black, hooded figure behind him slid a plastic bag over his head and pulled its corners tight. The muscles of the hooded figure's forearms bulged beneath its robes. Mario's body jerked and buckled.

Finally, two more hooded figures dragged a tall, coffin-like chest, connected to their bodies by linked chains. They opened the box to reveal the Princess, her body pierced by dozens, maybe hundreds, of steel spikes. Her torturers splashed acid on her and laughed as pixilated flesh sizzled and smoked.

These vile sounds and images went past his ears, into his brain and beyond that to his very soul. Like the Koopa Troopa in the other chamber, he felt hollowed out and dry. How could he save those he loved if they were already in such dire states?

"*It's just a movie*," he said to himself, over and over until he believed it. "*Just a movie*."

At room's end, there was no door, just a seemingly unbroken wall from which hung a knotty and irregular rope. Musclebound Mario approached the rope. Closer, he realized it was comprised of a line of corpses. The Goombas there had dried up, becoming mummies without bandages. Spineys had likewise fossilized. Koopa Troopas had been reduced to shell.

He took the corpse-rope in his hands. He started to climb and wasn't repulsed. The Goombas' skulls—with their huge, round eyeholes—looked especially like toys.

Then, halfway up, he found himself staring into the eyeholes of a dead Hammer Brother. Maggots writhed across broken teeth and inside empty sockets. Musclebound Mario hurled.

Wiping his lips, breathing through his nose, he struggled to climb past the thing. Hands and feet slid across and into the ruined body, reducing exposed parts to mush that smeared all over the hero and the husks to which he clung.

At the end of the corpse-rope, he heaved his body over a ledge. Before him: a precipice and a slide, torch-lit from the top but extending into total darkness.

He jumped onto the slide. His body traveled faster and faster, down and further down, and was nearly flung from the edge as the slide angled and curved before becoming steep. It sent the hero's body into a free-fall until its trajectory leveled out, and the slide ejected him into a blood red room.

In it: a lone Firebar. Beyond that: a bridge.

Arising, he built up speed to perform the highest jump he could manage without crushing his skull against the ceiling. That single leap took him to the center of the span.

He looked down, expecting lava but instead seeing molten game cartridges, their labels floating to the top, somehow unburned. Looking back up, he caught sight of the Nemesis, a figure as black as the tortures in the film, but its blackness was internal and, he feared, all-consuming.

Musclebound Mario prepared to attack. The Nemesis responded by accosting him with a wave of terror so sheer and dark that he could no longer scream, no longer feel, see or hear anything but the wave. It enveloped him, tried to suck him into itself and erase him.

Through squinted eyes, he saw the Nemesis flash dimly at regular intervals. During those flashes, it seemed there might be a body beneath the cloak. If he struck when the Nemesis was tangible, he would either lock it into a death-pattern or be sucked forever into its dark maw.

Undaunted, Musclebound Mario took to the air. He landed atop the Nemesis in the instant it started to flash. The villain cried out. Cringed. The hero had inflicted damage, but the Nemesis moved back and forth across the bridge as though on skates, making it difficult for him to keep balance and maintain rhythm.

The hero had a solution. Focusing, he felt the heat of a fireball warm his belly. But he wasn't satisfied to create only one. He continued to perform jumps and kept forming fireballs—hundreds and then thousands of them—until his stomach became a kiln and his throat a chimney that spat a constant barrage of flame at the thing's covered head.

Finding a pattern no longer mattered. The Nemesis's body flickered wildly. Following the hero's two hundred and fifty-thousandth fireball strike, it disintegrated into black pellets that fell to and skittered on and over the bridge like marbles.

Musclebound Mario sighed and wiped away sweat. It was over, and he had won. Now, where was the Princess?

Prince, he reminded himself, and felt his Mission Accomplished vibe fade slightly.

He moved to cross the bridge, like he knew he should. There was no chamber at its end, but a brown and white cartoon dog once hidden by the Nemesis. Hirsute body huge and towering, it glowered down at him with wide, unblinking eyes and laughed.

Something big slammed up against the hero's head. He'd seen nothing move. At that instant, images of a puny, sandy-haired boy, no more than 13, entered his headspace.

The boy sat on a bed, playing a videogame in which he had to shoot and kill ducks. When he missed, the same dog arose from the weeds. It laughed at this boy as it had laughed at the hero, opened its mouth wide and sucked him into the TV as though the set were the pot of a Piranha Plant.

The kid was spat into the bowels of a North American middle school. Down the boy's pants went, day after day. In civics class. In gym class. In study hall. In the cafeteria when he was holding a tray and had to walk to a table and put down the tray before pulling up his pants. Then he saw the boy's head thrust into a toilet, his locker pried open and the stuff in it strewn down a hall. He saw neighbor kids slip into his bedroom through an open window. They destroyed precious game cartridges with uncaring hands.

Such images seemed more real, direct and visceral than the wave of black malice the decoy had thrown at him. He wanted to hide his face. Break something. *Anything.* But why feel so strongly for things that had happened to a scrawny kid?

"A sad story," he said. "But is that all you can throw at me, you furry fuck?" He regretted saying this, for the Laughing Dog called his bluff, and visions again assailed his mind. The boy had returned, a little older and taller, but no happier. He was friendless, and those of the opposite sex ignored him. But he had learned to take solace in a game that came bundled with the one that featured the Laughing Dog. Once, it had simply been fun. Now, it was his god, and his awkward, teenaged body was an unworthy supplicant. It had to hit the gym so that the cornerstone to a future temple might soon be laid.

The flood of revelation continued until it seemed there were no more secrets. The thing had burrowed straight through to his psyche and unearthed from its rotten core nothing but disaffection, sorrow and loneliness.

And still the dog laughed and laughed, the sound worming past Musclebound Mario's ears and into his mind, soul and beyond, making him feel fat, stupid and useless. Like the boy in his fantasy, he had to deal with adversaries in his underwear, and those with pants tended to defeat those who had none.

Only rational thought could combat rampaging emotion. The hero struggled to bring such thoughts to mind and, once they came, latched tightly onto them.

Indeed, he reasoned, the things the dog shot at him were terrible, but they were just discombobulated images not unlike dreams. Not only that, the Laughing Dog was a glorified cartoon character while he was *Man*. Whatever power it had, he had fed to it, and it was within his power to walk away and never think of this non-entity again.

But he wasn't going to do that. He was going to pound the smugness out of its fat, hitching body.

Growling, Musclebound Mario launched himself at the Laughing Dog. He rammed his head into its stomach until the enemy collapsed. The hero straddled it, gripped its throat and banged its head against the bridge. "Die, you son of a bitch!" he exclaimed. "Die! Die! Die!"

The air around his right hand shimmered. He raised that hand from his opponent's neck—one was enough to throttle it—and opened his palm. A NES ZAPPER appeared in it. Words on the side spelled out KINGMAKER.

He stared at the weapon while thinking of a famous line from another game. He could either throw the gun away or use it. He decided to use it…to *finish* the Laughing Dog.

He pressed the trigger. The Laughing Dog shrieked as real-looking blood and guts exploded like shrapnel from its body. They coated the hero, and he smelled strange green and brown and orange and black scents he'd never before smelled. He got hard again, and this time felt no shame. The dog no longer moved, but he continued to fire at it, wasting the corpse even after nothing remained to shoot.

Musclebound Mario heard a noise like crinkling cellophane. He stopped firing. From a portal at the foot of the bridge came forth a line of minor villains. Their bodies were healed and reconstituted, eight-bit and one-dimensional. They wore smiles on bright and happy faces. When the portal closed, they crowded around Musclebound Mario, some rubbing his legs like cats, others hopping up and down as though trying to find a way into his arms.

When they began to sing, he was too fired-up from an endorphin rush to listen. Instead, he regarded his gun and turned it around in his hand; felt its weight. Looking up from it, he beheld the villains' bright and beatific faces and realized that—yes—he had to kill them, too.

Hefting the KINGMAKER, he fired it at the closest Goomba. Its happy smile was blown off its face and plastered to a wall. Next, he turned the zapper to the closest Koopa Troopa. Its entire body exploded in a blue-green blur from the back of its shell. The remaining villains scrambled but found no place to hide, and no mercy from Musclebound Mario. His finger depressed the trigger so rapidly that the surrounding plastic emitted steam and deformed.

In less than thirty seconds, all villains were dead, splayed across the floor, the scent of their spilled fluids and offal choking the air. Musclebound Mario breathed deeply the odor and threw the molten gun to the floor.

The hero heard footsteps. From the still-open portal, a familiar shape materialized. It was his old guide, but no longer was he merely Bowser. He was the crowned *King Koopa*.

"I am so very proud of you," the king said.

Musclebound Mario felt compelled to bow.

"Please, there's no need for that."

"But I—"

"But nothing. Arise now."

Slowly, the hero returned to his feet. "So, uh, is everything back to normal? Are you the bad guy again?"

"Not quite yet."

"Oh, okay. In that case, can I...uh...get your autograph? I asked earlier, but you weren't a king then."

He seemed to think. For a few painful seconds, it seemed he might refuse. Then a pen of white goose feather appeared in his hand. "But what should I sign? Ah!" A laminated 8x10 photo appeared in his other hand. "Want it personalized?"

"Please!"

King Koopa bent his head over the glossy. He signed with a flourish in the seconds before the quill pen vanished.

Smiling, the hero claimed the photo. He looked down; his smile vanished, too. King Koopa had dedicated the photo to the wrong person, and the image—a close-up headshot—was itself wrong.

"This isn't you." He tapped the photo. "I know this face. This is—"

King Koopa pulled down on a zipper now visible in the center of his forehead. Seconds later, the Creator stood before the hero. His hair was long and flowing. He was clad in a white robe.

"Mr. Miyamoto!" Musclebound Mario gasped and bowed again.

"Remember what I said about bowing?"

"But this time I must!" Then he tried to touch an exposed, sacred foot.

Quickly, the Creator swept his robe over the foot. "No, stand. *Look*. Choose to face me, my son."

"Your son?"

His smile was wider than the world. "I mean that as a term of endearment. You are your own creation, but I am the creator you favor most."

"I see," he said, though he really didn't see at all. "It's just—I don't know. God! I can't believe you're here again!"

"Did you think I'd leave you?"

"Honestly, I didn't know what to think."

The Creator's aura expanded to encase Musclebound Mario in a bubble, bright and iridescently blue. "I would never do that. We're friends."

Try as he might, and even inside the bubble, Musclebound Mario couldn't meet Mr. Miyamoto's gaze for more than a few moments.

"Don't be shy," the Creator said. "Again, I am proud. You have done well."

Musclebound Mario wanted to believe this, but he

had made so many missteps and gone down so many wrong paths. He doubted he deserved to be in the presence of greatness.

Mr. Miyamoto tousled his hair. His smile became a living lantern. "Everything's fine; trust me." He paused a beat. "But you aren't quite finished yet."

"What do you mean? Everybody's dead."

"Have you forgotten about the Prince?"

Musclebound Mario scratched the back of his neck. "Honestly, I haven't given him much thought."

"He is the reason you are here now."

"I never gave a crap about the Prince. It was always the game."

"Maybe so, but the game must end with its hero receiving a proper and satisfying reward."

Musclebound Mario sighed and reached for the still-steaming KINGMAKER on the floor. "Okay. I guess I'll kill him, too."

"No, no, no. You mustn't kill him. You must *kiss* him."

Musclebound Mario's skin prickled. "I must what?"

Mr. Miyamoto rolled his eyes. "Just do it, okay?"

"Okay, okay."

The Creator gestured to a previously non-existent door. It creaked open. An unseen orchestra struck up a tune heavy on brass and percussion. Musclebound Mario composed himself, stepped outside the Creator's warm, blue bubble and walked, as triumphantly as he could muster, into a dungeon that smelled of sweat, feces, urine and death. There were no windows, but wan and sickly-seeming light entered...somehow. In a far corner, the Prince sat, face cupped in his hands. His clothes were sopping wet tatters, trimmed with mold.

Musclebound Mario was loathed to see, much less kiss the man's face. After so long in this prison, was it gross like that of a zombie? All moist and wormy and skin peeling off?

He took a few more tentative steps toward the Prince. A bloated brown rat let loose a squeal as the hero stepped upon its back and splintered its spine.

The Prince looked up at him.

Musclebound Mario flinched. It was the boy from his visions, only he had grown into a man.

The Creator entered the dungeon and approached the hero. "Do you understand what you see?"

He pointed at the Prince. "That—that's a face I once thought I had."

"And it's a face you can have again. But tell me, are you ready to leave this world behind?"

"I… I, uh—I think so. I—"

"You don't sound sure. You *must* be sure."

Musclebound Mario considered this. Had he really been this Prince guy? Better yet, did he *want* to be him? The Prince wasn't a citizen of the Mushroom Kingdom. His place, the hero somehow knew, was one where things weren't so predictable, coins were harder to find and villains not so easily defeated. And there was no timer or soundtrack.

But there was unscripted possibility in his forever-mutable world, and that seemed to make all the difference.

"I've come this far," he said. "Guess I'd better accept."

The Creator smiled. "Then go kiss your Prince."

Hesitantly, skittishly, with the Creator walking purposely behind him, Musclebound Mario approached the Prince. The hero's mouth was slightly ajar, his chest tight and palms sweaty.

The Creator pushed his back to goad him onward.

The Prince regarded him with wide and expectant eyes.

Musclebound Mario sighed. "Guess we'd better do this," he said. Stooping then leaning forward, he kissed the Prince on the cheek. An electric spark bit his bottom lip as lightning flashed across the room.

"More!" the Creator demanded. "You must go deeper than that!"

"But I'm not sure I can. I—"

"Deeper, damn you!"

Musclebound Mario understood he had two choices: offer the Prince a penetrating soul kiss or spit upon destiny. Closing his eyes, he parted his lips. The other man parted his own and allowed the hero's tongue to enter and probe his mouth. The Prince's tongue did likewise, the tip of it eventually worming so far down the hero's throat that he gagged.

More lightning flashed. The Prince's hand clasped Musclebound Mario's. Fingertips first, his own hand entered that of the Prince.

Still, they kissed, even as his face and then the rest of his body began to slide into the other man. The lightning's flash became stroboscopic as sliver stars filled his vision. There was a singular sound, heavy and drum-like. The stars danced to it. His very molecules danced as well. It was as though the whole of the universe had become a bright, pulsing heart as the transit continued, reconstituting and refining them both until not three bodies stood in the room but two—the Creator and another that boasted the physique of Musclebound Mario and the face of the Prince.

The hero leaned against a damp stone wall, panting. Though neither original man had smoked, the entity that still thought of itself as Musclebound Mario would have taken a cigarette, had one been offered.

Almost a minute passed before he realized that the Creator was still in the room. "Oh hey," he said, voice warbling.

The Creator's smile wrapped around everything and felt warmer and more absorbing than the kiss. "It is done, and you are finally ready to complete your true mission." He reached into his pocket. "Here. Take this talisman."

It was gold. It glittered. It was shaped like a bejeweled baton.

"Is it lucky?" Musclebound Mario asked.

"Don't ask. Take."

The talisman throbbed like a heart in his hand.

"Now go forth with your glorified body, young man!" The Creator outstretched his arms. "Give yourself to the world! Right its wrongs!"

As if on vocal command, the wall nearest to him rumbled and slid opened. The hero exited the sphere of the Creator's smile and motioned to the breach. Passing through it, he found himself sheathed in darkness so total that it left residue on his skin. This made him remember he was only wearing underwear. Feeling vulnerable, he turned quickly. There was no trace of the room he'd left, or the Creator.

Dim passageways went on and on until it seemed that the entire world might be nothing but endless dim passageways. Through the gloom he stumbled, foul water from a moss-encrusted ceiling dripping on his head. He bumped into walls coated with green and yellow slime. His feet sank into brown muck.

It seemed things were moving fast above him— big and likely scary things. He wished he still had the KINGMAKER, but sensed its powers were negligible in this realm. Instead, he clutched the talisman tighter.

Tiny yellow eyes watched him from almost every corner. Their owners squeaked as if to say, *we don't want you here*. He didn't want to be here, either. Where was the world he'd been promised? Had the Creator lied to him, too?

Looking up at the ceiling, he noticed a break in the

darkness. It appeared as an outlined circle—a halo of light.

A ladder led to it. He climbed up dozens of slick and rusty rungs. At the top, he lifted a metal cap. Light flooded into his eyes. He craved more of that light, but the hole was too small for egress. Pressing himself against the ceiling, he strained until it broke open and he emerged onto a busy city street.

Car tires screeched. A grille and a hood wrapped around Musclebound Mario's lower extremities like leggings of twisted steel. He looked down at the windshield. A driver convulsed behind it. His face was crammed against the glass, lips contorted into a red smile.

"Aw shit!" the hero said. "Sorry, dude!"

He uncoiled the wreckage from his limbs. To avert continued damage, he hopped over the remaining lanes of cars to reach a bus stop. He stood there for a few seconds, seeing people stare, hearing others scream, until he remembered who he was and that he would never have to take public transportation again.

He shook his head to dislodge cobwebs. He needed to become acclimated to his new body—in this world, especially—so, placing the talisman under the waistband of his briefs, he raced away from onlookers, to a park where it seemed he might attract less attention.

There, he smashed into trash cans and crashed into fountains. Then he scared off a cadre of pigeons by looking at them crossly. Little things, but they provided him such joy and excitement.

Turning, he caught sight of a decorative brick archway. It brought to mind the one thing that he—or, now, a part of himself—had once exalted beyond all others. In seconds, happy memories of TV screens and controllers and the One True Game rushed back to him. Bathing in them, he sprinted over to the archway.

Coins, coins, coins. He beat his head on all the

bricks he could see. Though none offered him money, he continued until heaping piles of brick covered the sidewalk and someone behind him screamed.

Musclebound Mario ignored the distraction. He had spotted another interesting thing: a large flowerpot that held a small tree. He yanked the tree up by its roots and clamored atop the pot. The woman who had screamed earlier cowered on the ground—blubbering, red-eyed, hands scraping down her face—as he sank into the soil.

The hero surveyed the space in which he'd found himself. It provided yet another disappointment—just a bunch of dirt, fertilizer and worms. "No fucking coins!" he shouted. Throwing his arms to the side with frustration, he shattered the pot.

When shards fell away and dirt cleared, two men stood before him. One, stocky and broad-shouldered, was stone-faced, his eyes set in a cold stare. The other, smaller and thinner, was crouched behind his friend, bottom lip trembling.

"What the fuck are you?" the man out front demanded.

"I am—"

"I don't care what the fuck you are!"

"Then why did you ask?" Musclebound Mario boomed, air from his lungs blowing back the man's hair.

The man dismissed the question and pointed at the still-cowering bystander. "Can't you see you're scaring her? What kind of asshole scares a woman?"

"Calm down, Tom!" The smaller man took hold of the other's shoulder. "He looks crazy!"

Tom turned to his friend. "What? You don't think I can take him?"

"I—I don't know. I think he's some kind of monster."

"Shut up! You know I can take him!" He scowled. "And get your hand off me!"

"Okay! Okay!"

Tom addressed the hero. "Now, are you going to fuck off, or are you going to make me do something bad?"

Musclebound Mario sighed. "I don't get your problem. Just chill out, okay?"

"Chill out? Hell, I'm gonna waste your ass!" He produced a gun from a concealed holster. Grinning, he waved it in the air.

"What the shit, Tom?" said his paper-white friend. Then he reached for the gun as though to seize it.

Tom shoved the other man. "Never touch my gun!" he snapped.

"Please, put it away. Don't—"

"Shut up, you pussy! I have a permit!"

"But—"

"I said, *I have a permit!*"

Tom aimed the gun at the hero's head. At the sight of this, his friend took a step back and covered his face with both hands.

Musclebound Mario did not flinch. He realized there was no need to suffer this man. Still, he decided to give him one more chance. "Why be this way?" he said. "Is it because you need a gun to feel big like me?"

A vein in the center of the man's forehead fattened and pulsed. "Fuck you, you freak!" he shouted. Then he fired his gun.

Musclebound Mario caught the bullet and, without thinking, threw it back at him. The impact exploded the man's skull. His friend, coated in blood and brain matter, pissed himself as his mouth hung open in a silent scream.

"Oh fuck!" the hero said. Suddenly, there were sirens. No time for guilt. He jumped from the pot and bounded back toward the road.

Not a block from the park, cars with flashing lights surrounded him. Bowsers in Blue poured from them, fell into crouches and drew guns.

Before they could launch Bullet Bills into him, Musclebound Mario plowed through their ranks like a linebacker, grabbed each of their weapons and bent them into pretzel shapes. The remaining cops were dispersed with mighty sweeps of his hand.

Still, he heard sirens. His gaze fell on an empty newsstand kiosk. He uprooted it. Threw it at a cop car. The kiosk crashed into its hood, metal wrapping around and piercing metal until car and kiosk were one and the same. But other cops merely swerved out of the way, and there were so many of them now that it seemed only policemen drove in the city.

The hero began to feel outmatched. Outnumbered. Looking up and to his left, he glimpsed an aluminum five-pointed star that decorated the awning of a vacant store. He leapt up to absorb it, but it came unmoored from rusty hinges and crashed to the sidewalk. He refused to accept defeat. Gripping the star in both hands, he held it against his chest so tightly that metal deformed. Then he made a wish.

Chaotic music filled the air. Endorphins flooded Musclebound Mario's system. His eyes, veins and cock bulged. Rolling his stroboscopically flashing body into a ball, he took aim at the closest line of cars. On impact, the vehicles *plopped* and shot off like erupting popcorn kernels, some flung into buildings, others up into the sky, seemingly never to return. He repeated the act on nearby streets, sometimes following the road, other times taking shortcuts through walls, again and again, until he'd eliminated the threat.

Power continued to surge within him. Finally free to enjoy it, he wove through a host of fleeing pedestrians without upsetting their path. Then he slammed into a food cart and broke formation long enough to catch three hot dogs in his mouth. He chewed as he rolled up to and traversed the roof of a building, swallowed as he rolled back down to the street and into the path of tanker truck laden with skull-and-crossbones stickers.

The explosion forced Musclebound Mario from his coil, blew back his hair and flapped his jowls. Heat needled his skin but left it unburned. Instantly, exhilaration segued to dread as he imagined people blown to bits or buried beneath piles of rubble.

He didn't wait until the smoke cleared so that he might see what he'd wrought. He got into a crouch, and his subsequent jump sent him high into the sky.

From atop a multi-story building, Musclebound Mario made himself look at the huge crater in the street. Neighboring stores and apartment buildings lay in flame-licked ruins. Farther back, cop cars were imbedded in buildings. Survivors screamed and sobbed in streets. Above, news helicopter pilots dodged one another and angled for the best view.

He felt bad for regressing and causing such damage, but to dwell on past mistakes was a hindrance when the most vital mission of all remained unaccomplished. For the first time in his life, he was to be a hero in the one world that mattered.

As he bounded from rooftop to rooftop, en route to destiny, the Mario-head peeled from the front of his briefs and came to rest facedown in a trashcan. At that moment, he thought of the talisman. Grabbing the dry, brown turd, he tossed it away. It meant nothing to him, for he was Musclebound Marcus, and he would free a Princess not from a dungeon, but from a false king.

PART EIGHT: MUSCLEBOUND MARCUS

Musclebound Marcus stomped up to the property line of the party house, inadvertently flattening a poodle that had wandered into his path. He neither saw nor felt its demise. His attention was honed on the house. Before, it had seemed like such an imposing structure. Nearly magical. It felt like nothing now. Just a shell. Dead on the inside and out.

He entered the yard, crushed the mailbox and kicked the tail end of a car into the front end of another. Both were launched at the house, decimating the porch and leaving a yawning hole where the door had been.

He barreled his way past that hole, sideswiping someone dressed as a Bullet Bill. The partygoer shot across the room and took out a stereo system before crashing through not one wall, but two.

Brave Goombas, Koopa Troopas and Piranha Plants surrounded and tried to restrain him, slap him, or beat him with their fists. He knocked them, one by one, so that they smashed into and bowled over more cowardly revelers who scurried and screamed over spilled food and drink.

A butter knife wielding Bob-omb rushed him. The man's bellow turned into a long, shrill whine when Musclebound Marcus took him by the hips, hoisted him up over his shoulders and tossed him into the center of the illuminated Mario head. It didn't hurt the hero to see its face obliterated. It was a flimsy prop.

Across the hall, a door was flung open. Bowser guards emerged and charged at him. Swung their axes. Missed. Seizing their bodies, Musclebound Marcus spun them so that they faced one another, then grabbed them both by the hair and crashed their heads together with the force he'd deemed necessary to knock them out cold.

He hadn't gauged correctly. Skulls exploded. Blood and brains covered his hands, face and body. He could fret over this later. Musclebound Marcus shook off the viscera as he panned his gaze across the room.

Fewer than ten partygoers remained, cowering behind a sideways buffet table in costumes that appeared more sad than awesome. He lifted his foot to show all in attendance its size 60 sole. "Get out before I smash you to hell!" he shouted.

The crowd broke in haste, but a single guest dressed as Wario remained where he stood. "Can I, uh, stay?" he said.

Incredulous, Musclebound Marcus gave no reply.

"Can we, you know, be a team, or can I at least get your autograph?"

"No, you son of a bitch! Leave!"

There was more scurrying, and he spotted someone run from the kitchen, someone who pretended to be a Goomba, only he wore a poster board sign emblazoned with a large, blood-red S. Gradually, he recalled a name.

Pointing at Tim, he said, "Not you. You stay."

"But—"

"*You stay!*"

The man froze. Said nothing.

"Come closer! *Now!*"

Tim appeared ready to swoon. Musclebound Marcus ran to him, caught him before he could fall, but the man wouldn't make eye contact. Instead, he locked an unblinking stare on the wall and trembled like a tiny, nervous dog.

Musclebound Marcus bared his teeth and roared, "Look into my eyes, motherfucker!"

The motherfucker looked into his eyes. "Are you— going to kill me?"

Musclebound Marcus seemed to consider this. Finally, he said, "Nah, man. I just want you to know that you're a total fucking asshole." He smiled. "And I want you to say it, too."

His lips moved. No words came out.

"*Say it*!"

"I'm a total fucking asshole."

"Good, but say it again. Mean it this time."

"*I'm a total fucking asshole*!"

Musclebound Marcus' smile widened. "You bet you are."

Tim still quaked, but appeared hopeful. "Is—is that all?"

"Yeah. That's all. Get the fuck out."

The man scrambled. Musclebound Marcus noticed the piss stain on the front of his costume and felt only slightly guilty for having gloated.

Bending down, he picked up one of the Bowser guard corpses. He held it by its ankles as he dragged it into the hall and tore the door to the throne room from its hinges. The passage was too small to enter, so he pushed his way through the wall itself. Timbers and drywall flecked with paint clung to his flesh and tattered briefs.

The Princess was in the midst of running into a closet. The king, at that moment shouting into a cell phone, recoiled in his throne so violently it nearly toppled. "You!" he shouted. "It cannot be!"

Musclebound Marcus lunged. In a blind panic, the king tried to retreat further into the cushion. With a free hand, the hero seized the pretender, lifted him until his head met the ceiling and dashed him to the floor.

The king was in a fetal position. "No, please!" he said. "I—I—won't say a thing! And I'll—I'll—"

Musclebound Marcus lofted the dead guard over his head like a club.

"And I'll lift the ban! I swear it! Really! I—"

Over and over, the hero brought the corpse-bat down on the king's upper body. Briefly, he saw the man's face as that of a broken and dying Laughing Dog, which caused him to strike harder.

Something stirred within him. He stopped hammering. A tingle that began in his chest became a pulse that became an insistent, full-body throb that electrified him and stood his every hair on end. He felt that he should flap his arms. When he did, he arose from the floor.

In ecstasy at having Powered Up on his own terms, he flew circles around the room. In time, he grew bored, so he smashed through the window, flying first below the trees before gaining the confidence to soar to a height where he looked down and could see the world as a vast plane of lines and dots atop a grid. There, he realized he didn't have to flap his arms to remain aloft.

A bird passed him. "Hey," he said, wondering where the bird was going and if he should follow, but then realized he'd forgotten something important:

The Princess.

He descended so rapidly that his ears popped. Landing back in house, he saw her bowed over the king, rocking slightly, her back to the hero.

"Need him," she said, voice a reedy whisper.

Musclebound Marcus sidled up to her, stroked her hair. "No, you don't. You never did."

"Need him," she repeated.

He leaned to the right so that her face became visible.

The surgical pixelation had robbed her of the subtly of expression, but he could see within her eyes a vacancy that unnerved him and made him feel culpable.

"Sorry for all the mess, Princess, but nothing can hurt us anymore. We're both free."

She said nothing. Just stared down at the now and forever dead king.

He sighed. There had to be something he could do, something that would burst her out of this sad bubble and allow her to finally become the Princess she was born to be. Then, in a flash of inspiration, the solution came to him.

He reached out for the Princess, and she tried half-heartedly to smack him away, but he came at her again, took her into his grasp and stood.

"Hold on tight," he said, but the Princess' arms dangled limply to her sides as he shot past the ceiling and out the roof, careful to shield her from debris with his arms and bowed head.

The sky embraced them. The wind blew her hair into a rich, golden fan. "Thank you so much for saving me, Musclebound Marcus," he wanted her to say to him. It seemed fitting. But she moaned and said, almost inaudibly, "Back. Take me…back."

Perhaps he needed to travel higher. Impress her with sheer altitude. But she would require protection first, so he willed his aura to solidify and expand, encasing them both in a force field. Then he shifted his westward pointing body to aim at the clouds. Like a rocket, he soared toward them. The sound barrier was broken with a noise heard by thousands.

He looked down. It seemed there was nothing, not even clouds, below him. He looked up and beheld the moon growing ever larger. They'd be there soon. He could stop, spend time exploring the lunar surface with the Princess and give her moon rock souvenirs. But no, he wasn't content to tour such a dull and lifeless place. It didn't reflect his mood.

Instead, he flew to the stars.

But even they seemed like little more than glorified Christmas decor, so he refused to stop at them as well. His energy was inexhaustible. He traveled faster than the speed of light. Now, there were no stars. Just a void that seemed eternal. But he felt no fear or trepidation. In fact, he sensed there might be something beyond nothing, and he would keep going until he defied the odds and discovered infinity's end.

In time, the void became…something else, and he found that he could walk rather than fly. There was a door before him, hanging without hinges in otherwise empty space. He clutched the knob. Turned it. A great Hall of Records was revealed. Vaulted glass ceilings. Obsidian floors. Marble columns. Leather-bound tomes in shelves like skyscrapers. But he didn't need to open a single book to gain understanding. Time travel. Zero-point energy. Resurrection of the dead. The knowledge of everything was at his command.

But knowledge alone bored him. He blasted past this hall, back into the void and beyond to a place-that-wasn't-yet-was. There, his hair grew out and became a flowing Technicolor rainbow. His skin became like mercury from a broken thermometer. A breastplate locked over his chest; a matching codpiece cupped his scrotum and cock. In his left hand, a trident appeared as thick, bronze bracelets coiled about that arm like serpents. He remembered then that he held the Princess in the other arm. Her plastic crown had transmuted to one of platinum and jewels. She wore a cape of gold. Slippers of glass. Still, her face was slack. Eyes empty. Gone.

Musclebound Marcus frowned. He began to resent her blindness and lack of gratitude.

Ahead of him was another door, one that perhaps led into *all* rooms. Above and to the sides of it was a series of warning signs:

TURN BACK.
LEAVE NOW.
GO HOME.
YOU WILL NOT SURVIVE.

He ignored them, vowing to open that door and not be waylaid by anyone or anything. He reached it, threw it open but was unable to pass. A final sign, as large as the door, blocked his entry and resisted any pressure he exerted against it.

ONLY ONE MAY ENTER, it said.

Musclebound Marcus looked down at the Princess. Forced a smile. "You'll be okay," he said, though he doubted she'd heard him. Then he separated a portion of his aura-shield so that it enveloped her like an eggshell. "Just stay in this, alright?"

Her eyes regained a scintilla of lost clarity. "W-what?"

"It's not you, really. It's me." He released her to sail away. Her mouth fell open with the horror of understanding, and she kicked her feet and slammed her fists against the shell, but Musclebound Marcus saw none of this. He had returned his attention to the door.

The sign rolled up like a window shade. Beyond it, stars were birthed *ex niliho* and joined together, melding to the form the planet-sized head of Mr. Miyamoto. The Creator's face shone with bright and fierce malevolence. Stunned, Musclebound Marcus could only glimpse it through the corner of his left eye, which teared up with blood.

The Creator's mouth opened into a ring of fire. He puffed out his cheeks and blew the ring toward Musclebound Marcus. The hero ducked but his scalp burned. He smelled the stench of singed hair.

"Why, Mr. Miyamoto? I thought we were friends!"

His voice boomed with the force of colliding stars. "No, we are equals, and I abide no equals!"

A part of Musclebound Marcus wanted to protest, to

say that it could never do battle with something once exalted. But that part was withering, dying, and he had grown weary of betrayals. If the Creator wanted a battle, then a battle he would get.

Musclebound Marcus regarded his new trident. Perhaps he could put it to good use. He imagined laser beams shooting rapid-fire from its tip, striking the Creator and setting him ablaze. Immediately, the trident glowed; lasers shot from it, but when they hit him, Mr. Miyamoto laughed.

"Do better next time," he said, and opened his eyes wide. From the pupils came rotating circular saw blades. The hero spun his trident lengthwise, deflecting them, before he turned it to Mr. Miyamoto and materialized the first thing that entered his mind.

A net sailed across empty space as if blown by wind. The hero imagined it wrapping and shrinking around the Creator, compacting him into a ball small enough to be kicked out of reality.

Instead, he shook it away with a twist of his disembodied head. "What?" he said. "Am I a fish?" Then he brought into being a Mario doll larger than most stars, the top of the hat threaded with a lit fuse. Unshaken, the hero shot a beam from the trident, detonating the bomb before it could travel far from Mr. Miyamoto. The explosion blackened the Creator's face. Opening his mouth, he sent a long, bi-forked tongue in circles to clean off the soot.

"Oh well," he said. "It was worth a try."

Musclebound Marcus thought hard. He had to get creative, too. Seconds later, a pink-scaled, blue-eyed dragon emerged fully formed from the trident. It raced up to the Creator on thick, muscular legs and blew gouts of fire. The Creator opened his mouth, sucked in the fire and blew it back at the dragon, incinerating it.

Frustration mounted. Musclebound Marcus gritted

his teeth and visualized all the weaponry he could conceive. Grenades and bombs and bullets and knives and clubs and anvils and even sticks and stones shot *en masse* from the trident. Their collective bulk obscured Mr. Miyamoto from view.

When the storm cleared, the Creator remained, but his head was a perfect circle, face stretched and widened, like it had been painted upon a balloon prior to inflation. Eyes huge, nose bulbous, lips forced into a grin, the sight of him would have been comical had Musclebound Marcus not grasped the implication.

"Game over," said the Creator, and shot forth the weapons he'd amassed as a gargantuan ball of black energy. It came at the hero too fast to avoid. There was an impact, and then immense pain, like a thousand deaths experienced without dying. Still, he tightened his muscles, his resolve, and made himself hold the energy in his body, too.

He could return the energy, but the Creator would shoot it back and forth at him—an endless cycle. At that moment, he recalled Musclebound Luigi's phony sacrifice and saw the path he must take. Proudly and without blinking, he stared straight into the face of the Creator. He smiled despite his hemorrhaging eyes.

Centering himself, he collected all his hopes and dreams, failures and successes, loves and hates in the pit of his stomach where he honed them, sharpened them, mourned for and said goodbye to them. Then he added them to the energy ball, leaving within him only enough power to initiate launch.

He aimed his naval. Fired. The ball, deep red, blasted from him. The Creator could only watch, mouth ajar, as it soared. The ball struck his nose and, like a stone in mud, sank slowly, pulling facial features and the rest of Mr Miyamoto down into a vortex. Screams of agony rent holes through space-time. Inner light dimming, he collapsed in on himself.

An expended Musclebound Marcus was sucked into a hole and shattered. His particles blasted out like comets in every direction and burned brighter than the morning star. Space expanded to accommodate him; time cooled him. Protons, neutron and electrons gathered in clouds, reforming matter. It attracted itself. Compacted. Stars shone and galaxies swirled on the great canvas of his body. Soon, there was water. Soon, there was life. Legends were written and tales were told of him long after his day, and Musclebound Marcus was reborn with each telling.

THE END

Defying polar vortex. Trust me, the underwear is red.

Apparently, Kevin L. Donihe prefers briefs over boxers. He has published over ten books via Eraserhead Press. His short fiction and poetry has appeared in *Psychos: Serial Killers, Depraved Madmen, and the Criminally Insane, The Mammoth Book of Legal Thrillers, ChiZine, The Cafe Irreal, Not One of Us, Dreams and Nightmares, Electric Velocipede, The Best Bizarro Fiction of the Decade* and other venues. He also edited the Bare Bone anthology series for Raw Dog Screaming Press, a story from which was reprinted in *The Mammoth Book of Best New Horror 13*. Visit him online at facebook.com/kevin.l.donihe

BIZARRO BOOKS

CATALOG   SPRING 2013

ERASERHEAD PRESS

Your major resource for the bizarro fiction genre:

WWW.BIZARROCENTRAL.COM

Introduce yourselves to the bizarro fiction genre and all of its authors with the Bizarro Starter Kit series. Each volume features short novels and short stories by ten of the leading bizarro authors, designed to give you a perfect sampling of the genre for only $10.

BB-0X1
"The Bizarro Starter Kit" (Orange)
Featuring D. Harlan Wilson, Carlton Mellick III, Jeremy Robert Johnson, Kevin L Donihe, Gina Ranalli, Andre Duza, Vincent W. Sakowski, Steve Beard, John Edward Lawson, and Bruce Taylor.
236 pages $10

BB-0X2
"The Bizarro Starter Kit" (Blue)
Featuring Ray Fracalossy, Jeremy C. Shipp, Jordan Krall, Mykle Hansen, Andersen Prunty, Eckhard Gerdes, Bradley Sands, Steve Aylett, Christian TeBordo, and Tony Rauch. **244 pages $10**

BB-0X2
"The Bizarro Starter Kit" (Purple)
Featuring Russell Edson, Athena Villaverde, David Agranoff, Matthew Revert, Andrew Goldfarb, Jeff Burk, Garrett Cook, Kris Saknussemm, Cody Goodfellow, and Cameron Pierce **264 pages $10**

BB-001 **"The Kafka Effekt" D. Harlan Wilson** — A collection of forty-four irreal short stories loosely written in the vein of Franz Kafka, with more than a pinch of William S. Burroughs sprinkled on top. **211 pages $14**

BB-002 **"Satan Burger" Carlton Mellick III** — The cult novel that put Carlton Mellick III on the map ... Six punks get jobs at a fast food restaurant owned by the devil in a city violently overpopulated by surreal alien cultures. **236 pages $14**

BB-003 **"Some Things Are Better Left Unplugged" Vincent Sakwoski** — Join The Man and his Nemesis, the obese tabby, for a nightmare roller coaster ride into this postmodern fantasy. **152 pages $10**

BB-005 **"Razor Wire Pubic Hair" Carlton Mellick III** — A genderless humandildo is purchased by a razor dominatrix and brought into her nightmarish world of bizarre sex and mutilation. **176 pages $11**

BB-007 **"The Baby Jesus Butt Plug" Carlton Mellick III** — Using clones of the Baby Jesus for anal sex will be the hip sex fetish of the future. **92 pages $10**

BB-010 **"The Menstruating Mall" Carlton Mellick III** — "The Breakfast Club meets Chopping Mall as directed by David Lynch." - Brian Keene **212 pages $12**

BB-011 **"Angel Dust Apocalypse" Jeremy Robert Johnson** — Meth-heads, man-made monsters, and murderous Neo-Nazis. "Seriously amazing short stories..." - Chuck Palahniuk, author of Fight Club **184 pages $11**

BB-015 **"Foop!" Chris Genoa** — Strange happenings are going on at Dactyl, Inc, the world's first and only time travel tourism company.
"A surreal pie in the face!" - Christopher Moore **300 pages $14**

BB-032 **"Extinction Journals" Jeremy Robert Johnson** — An uncanny voyage across a newly nuclear America where one man must confront the problems associated with loneliness, insane dieties, radiation, love, and an ever-evolving cockroach suit with a mind of its own. **104 pages $10**

BB-037 **"The Haunted Vagina" Carlton Mellick III** — It's difficult to love a woman whose vagina is a gateway to the world of the dead. **132 pages $10**

BB-043 **"War Slut" Carlton Mellick III** — Part "1984," part "Waiting for Godot," and part action horror video game adaptation of John Carpenter's "The Thing." **116 pages $10**

BB-047 **"Sausagey Santa" Carlton Mellick III** — A bizarro Christmas tale featuring Santa as a piratey mutant with a body made of sausages. **124 pages $10**

BB-048 **"Misadventures in a Thumbnail Universe" Vincent Sakowski** — Dive deep into the surreal and satirical realms of neo-classical Blender Fiction, filled with television shoes and flesh-filled skies. **120 pages $10**

BB-053 **"Ballad of a Slow Poisoner" Andrew Goldfarb** — Millford Mutterwurst sat down on a Tuesday to take his afternoon tea, and made the unpleasant discovery that his elbows were becoming flatter. **128 pages $10**

BB-055 **"Help! A Bear is Eating Me" Mykle Hansen** — The bizarro, heartwarming, magical tale of poor planning, hubris and severe blood loss... **150 pages $11**

BB-056 **"Piecemeal June" Jordan Krall** — A man falls in love with a living sex doll, but with love comes danger when her creator comes after her with crab-squid assassins. **90 pages $9**

BB-058 **"The Overwhelming Urge" Andersen Prunty** — A collection of bizarro tales by Andersen Prunty. **150 pages $11**

BB-059 **"Adolf in Wonderland" Carlton Mellick III** — A dreamlike adventure that takes a young descendant of Adolf Hitler's design and sends him down the rabbit hole into a world of imperfection and disorder. **180 pages $11**

BB-061 **"Ultra Fuckers" Carlton Mellick III** — Absurdist suburban horror about a couple who enter an upper middle class gated community but can't find their way out. **108 pages $9**

BB-062 **"House of Houses" Kevin L. Donihe** — An odd man wants to marry his house. Unfortunately, all of the houses in the world collapse at the same time in the Great House Holocaust. Now he must travel to House Heaven to find his departed fiancee. **172 pages $11**

BB-064 **"Squid Pulp Blues" Jordan Krall** — In these three bizarro-noir novellas, the reader is thrown into a world of murderers, drugs made from squid parts, deformed gun-toting veterans, and a mischievous apocalyptic donkey. **204 pages $12**

BB-065 **"Jack and Mr. Grin" Andersen Prunty** — "When Mr. Grin calls you can hear a smile in his voice. Not a warm and friendly smile, but the kind that seizes your spine in fear. You don't need to pay your phone bill to hear it. That smile is in every line of Prunty's prose." - Tom Bradley. **208 pages $12**

BB-066 **"Cybernetrix" Carlton Mellick III** — What would you do if your normal everyday world was slowly mutating into the video game world from Tron? **212 pages $12**

BB-072 **"Zerostrata" Andersen Prunty** — Hansel Nothing lives in a tree house, suffers from memory loss, has a very eccentric family, and falls in love with a woman who runs naked through the woods every night. **144 pages $11**

BB-073 **"The Egg Man" Carlton Mellick III** — It is a world where humans reproduce like insects. Children are the property of corporations, and having an enormous ten-foot brain implanted into your skull is a grotesque sexual fetish. Mellick's industrial urban dystopia is one of his darkest and grittiest to date. **184 pages $11**

BB-074 **"Shark Hunting in Paradise Garden" Cameron Pierce** — A group of strange humanoid religious fanatics travel back in time to the Garden of Eden to discover it is invested with hundreds of giant flying maneating sharks. **150 pages $10**

BB-075 **"Apeshit" Carlton Mellick III -** Friday the 13th meets Visitor Q. Six hipster teens go to a cabin in the woods inhabited by a deformed killer. An incredibly fucked-up parody of B-horror movies with a bizarro slant. **192 pages $12**

BB-076 **"Fuckers of Everything on the Crazy Shitting Planet of the Vomit At smosphere" Mykle Hansen -** Three bizarro satires. Monster Cocks, Journey to the Center of Agnes Cuddlebottom, and Crazy Shitting Planet. **228 pages $12**

BB-077 **"The Kissing Bug" Daniel Scott Buck** — In the tradition of Roald Dahl, Tim Burton, and Edward Gorey, comes this bizarro anti-war children's story about a bohemian conenose kissing bug who falls in love with a human woman. **116 pages $10**

BB-078 **"MachoPoni" Lotus Rose** — It's My Little Pony... *Bizarro* style! A long time ago Poniworld was split in two. On one side of the Jagged Line is the Pastel Kingdom, a magical land of music, parties, and positivity. On the other side of the Jagged Line is Dark Kingdom inhabited by an army of undead ponies. **148 pages $11**

BB-079 **"The Faggiest Vampire" Carlton Mellick III** — A Roald Dahl-esque children's story about two faggy vampires who partake in a mustache competition to find out which one is truly the faggiest. **104 pages $10**

BB-080 **"Sky Tongues" Gina Ranalli** — The autobiography of Sky Tongues, the biracial hermaphrodite actress with tongues for fingers. Follow her strange life story as she rises from freak to fame. **204 pages $12**

BB-081 **"Washer Mouth" Kevin L. Donihe** - A washing machine becomes human and pursues his dream of meeting his favorite soap opera star. **244 pages $11**

BB-082 **"Shatnerquake" Jeff Burk** - All of the characters ever played by William Shatner are suddenly sucked into our world. Their mission: hunt down and destroy the real William Shatner. **100 pages $10**

BB-083 **"The Cannibals of Candyland" Carlton Mellick III** - There exists a race of cannibals that are made of candy. They live in an underground world made out of candy. One man has dedicated his life to killing them all. **170 pages $11**

BB-084 **"Slub Glub in the Weird World of the Weeping Willows"** **Andrew Goldfarb** - The charming tale of a blue glob named Slub Glub who helps the weeping willows whose tears are flooding the earth. There are also hyenas, ghosts, and a voodoo priest **100 pages $10**

BB-085 **"Super Fetus" Adam Pepper** - Try to abort this fetus and he'll kick your ass! **104 pages $10**

BB-086 **"Fistful of Feet" Jordan Krall** - A bizarro tribute to spaghetti westerns, featuring Cthulhu-worshipping Indians, a woman with four feet, a crazed gunman who is obsessed with sucking on candy, Syphilis-ridden mutants, sexually transmitted tattoos, and a house devoted to the freakiest fetishes. **228 pages $12**

BB-087 **"Ass Goblins of Auschwitz" Cameron Pierce** - It's Monty Python meets Nazi exploitation in a surreal nightmare as can only be imagined by Bizarro author Cameron Pierce. **104 pages $10**

BB-088 **"Silent Weapons for Quiet Wars" Cody Goodfellow** - "This is high-end psychological surrealist horror meets bottom-feeding low-life crime in a techno-thrilling science fiction world full of Lovecraft and magic..." -John Skipp **212 pages $12**

BB-089 **"Warrior Wolf Women of the Wasteland" Carlton Mellick III**
— Road Warrior Werewolves versus McDonaldland Mutants...post-apocalyptic fiction has never been quite like this. **316 pages $13**

BB-091 **"Super Giant Monster Time" Jeff Burk** — A tribute to choose your own adventures and Godzilla movies. Will you escape the giant monsters that are rampaging the fuck out of your city and shit? Or will you join the mob of alien-controlled punk rockers causing chaos in the streets? What happens next depends on you. **188 pages $12**

BB-092 **"Perfect Union" Cody Goodfellow** — "Cronenberg's THE FLY on a grand scale: human/insect gene-spliced body horror, where the human hive politics are as shocking as the gore." -John Skipp. **272 pages $13**

BB-093 **"Sunset with a Beard" Carlton Mellick III** — 14 stories of surreal science fiction. **200 pages $12**

BB-094 **"My Fake War" Andersen Prunty** — The absurd tale of an unlikely soldier forced to fight a war that, quite possibly, does not exist. It's Rambo meets Waiting for Godot in this subversive satire of American values and the scope of the human imagination. **128 pages $11**

BB-095 **"Lost in Cat Brain Land" Cameron Pierce** — Sad stories from a surreal world. A fascist mustache, the ghost of Franz Kafka, a desert inside a dead cat. Primordial entities mourn the death of their child. The desperate serve tea to mysterious creatures. A hopeless romantic falls in love with a pterodactyl. And much more. **152 pages $11**

BB-096 **"The Kobold Wizard's Dildo of Enlightenment +2" Carlton Mellick III** — A Dungeons and Dragons parody about a group of people who learn they are only made up characters in an AD&D campaign and must find a way to resist their nerdy teenaged players and retarded dungeon master in order to survive. **232 pages $12**

BB-098 **"A Hundred Horrible Sorrows of Ogner Stump" Andrew Goldfarb** — Goldfarb's acclaimed comic series. A magical and weird journey into the horrors of everyday life. **164 pages $11**

BB-099 "Pickled Apocalypse of Pancake Island" Cameron Pierce—A demented fairy tale about a pickle, a pancake, and the apocalypse. **102 pages $8**

BB-100 "Slag Attack" Andersen Prunty— Slag Attack features four visceral, noir stories about the living, crawling apocalypse. A slag is what survivors are calling the slug-like maggots raining from the sky, burrowing inside people, and hollowing out their flesh and their sanity. **148 pages $11**

BB-101 "Slaughterhouse High" Robert Devereaux—A place where schools are built with secret passageways, rebellious teens get zippers installed in their mouths and genitals, and once a year, on that special night, one couple is slaughtered and the bits of their bodies are kept as souvenirs. **304 pages $13**

BB-102 "The Emerald Burrito of Oz" John Skipp & Marc Levinthal —OZ IS REAL! Magic is real! The gate is really in Kansas! And America is finally allowing Earth tourists to visit this weird-ass, mysterious land. But when Gene of Los Angeles heads off for summer vacation in the Emerald City, little does he know that a war is brewing...a war that could destroy both worlds. **280 pages $13**

BB-103 "The Vegan Revolution... with Zombies" David Agranoff — When there's no more meat in hell, the vegans will walk the earth. **160 pages $11**

BB-104 "The Flappy Parts" Kevin L Donihe—Poems about bunnies, LSD, and police abuse. You know, things that matter. 132 **pages $11**

BB-105 "Sorry I Ruined Your Orgy" Bradley Sands—Bizarro humorist Bradley Sands returns with one of the strangest, most hilarious collections of the year. **130 pages $11**

BB-106 "Mr. Magic Realism" Bruce Taylor—Like Golden Age science fiction comics written by Freud, *Mr. Magic Realism* is a strange, insightful adventure that spans the furthest reaches of the galaxy, exploring the hidden caverns in the hearts and minds of men, women, aliens, and biomechanical cats. **152 pages $11**

BB-107 **"Zombies and Shit" Carlton Mellick III**—"Batt e Roya e" meets "Return of the Living Dead." Mellick's bizarro tribute to the zombie genre **308 pages $13**

BB-108 **"The Cannibal's Guide to Ethical Living" Mykle Hansen**— Over a five star French meal of fine wine, organic vegetables and human fle h, a lunatic delivers a witty, chilling, disturbingly sane argument in favor of eating the rich.. **184 pages $11**

BB-109 **"Starfish Girl" Athena Villaverde**—In a post-apoca yptic ur derwater dome society, a girl with a starfish growing from her head and an assas in with sea anenome hair are on the run from a gang of mutant fish men. **160 pages $11**

BB-110 **"Lick Your Neighbor" Chris Genoa**—Mutant ninjas a talking whale, kung fu masters, maniacal pilgrims, and an alcoholic clown populate Chri Genoa's surreal, darkly comical and unnerving reimagining of the first Thanksgiving. **303 pages $13**

BB-111 **"Night of the Assholes" Kevin L. Donihe**—A plague of assholes is infecting the countryside. Normal everyday people are transforming nto jerks, snobs, dicks, and douchebags. And they all have only one purpose: to make your life a li ing hell.. **192 pages $11**

BB-112 **"Jimmy Plush, Teddy Bear Detective" Garrett Cook**—Hardboiled cases of a private detective trapped within a teddy bear body. **180 pages $11**

BB-113 **"The Deadheart Shelters" Forrest Armstrong**—The hip hop lovechild of William Burroughs and Dali... **144 pages $11**

BB-114 **"Eyeballs Growing All Over Me... Again" Tony Raugh**— Absurd, surreal, playful, dream-like, whimsical, and a lot of fun to read. **144 pages $11**

BB-115 "Whargoul" Dave Brockie — From the killing grounds of Stalingrad to the death camps of the holocaust. From torture chambers in Iraq to race riots in the United States, the Whargoul was there, killing and raping. **244 pages $12**

BB-116 "By the Time We Leave Here, We'll Be Friends" J. David Osborne — A David Lynchian nightmare set in a Russian gulag, where its prisoners, guards, traitors, soldiers, lovers, and demons fight for survival and their own rapidly deteriorating humanity. **168 pages $11**

BB-117 "Christmas on Crack" edited by Carlton Mellick III — Perverted Christmas Tales for the whole family! . . . as long as every member of your family is over the age of 18. **168 pages $11**

BB-118 "Crab Town" Carlton Mellick III — Radiation fetishists, balloon people, mutant crabs, sail-bike road warriors, and a love affair between a woman and an H-Bomb. This is one mean asshole of a city. Welcome to Crab Town. **100 pages $8**

BB-119 "Rico Slade Will Fucking Kill You" Bradley Sands — Rico Slade is an action hero. Rico Slade can rip out a throat with his bare hands. Rico Slade's favorite food is the honey-roasted peanut. Rico Slade will fucking kill everyone. A novel. **122 pages $8**

BB-120 "Sinister Miniatures" Kris Saknussemm — The definitive collection of short fiction by Kris Saknussemm, confirming that he is one of the best, most daring writers of the weird to emerge in the twenty-first century. **180 pages $11**

BB-121 "Baby's First Book of Seriously Fucked up Shit" Robert Devereaux — Ten stories of the strange, the gross, and the just plain fucked up from one of the most original voices in horror. **176 pages $11**

BB-122 "The Morbidly Obese Ninja" Carlton Mellick III — These days, if you want to run a successful company . . . you're going to need a lot of ninjas. **92 pages $8**

BB-123 **"Abortion Arcade" Cameron Pierce** — An intoxicating blend of body horror and midnight movie madness, reminiscent of early David Lynch and the splatterpunks at their most sublime. **172 pages $11**

BB-124 **"Black Hole Blues" Patrick Wensink** — A hilarious double helix of country music and physics. **196 pages $11**

BB-125 **"Barbarian Beast Bitches of the Badlands" Carlton Mellick III** — Three prequels and sequels to *Warrior Wolf Women of the Wasteland.* **284 pages $13**

BB-126 **"The Traveling Dildo Salesman" Kevin L. Donihe** — A nightmare comedy about destiny, faith, and sex toys. Also featuring Donihe's most lurid and infamous short stories: *Milky Agitation, Two-Way Santa, The Helen Mower, Living Room Zombies,* and *Revenge of the Living Masturbation Rag.* **108 pages $8**

BB-127 **"Metamorphosis Blues" Bruce Taylor** — Enter a land of love beasts, intergalactic cowboys, and rock 'n roll. A land where Sears Catalogs are doorways to insanity and men keep mysterious black boxes. Welcome to the monstrous mind of Mr. Magic Realism. **136 pages $11**

BB-128 **"The Driver's Guide to Hitting Pedestrians" Andersen Prunty** — A pocket guide to the twenty-three most painful things in life, written by the most well-adjusted man in the universe. **108 pages $8**

BB-129 **"Island of the Super People" Kevin Shamel** — Four students and their anthropology professor journey to a remote island to study its indigenous population. But this is no ordinary native culture. They're super heroes and villains with flesh costumes and out-landish abilities like self-detonation, musical eyelashes, and microwave hands. **194 pages $11**

BB-130 **"Fantastic Orgy" Carlton Mellick III** — Shark Sex, mutant cats, and strange sexually transmitted diseases. Featuring the stories: *Candy-coated, Ear Cat, Fantastic Orgy, City Hobgoblins,* and *Porno in August.* **136 pages $9**

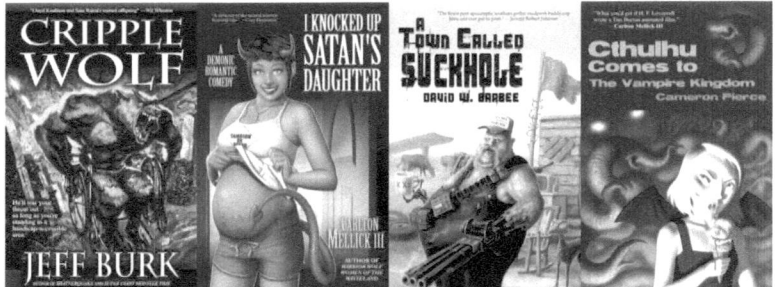

BB-131 **"Cripple Wolf" Jeff Burk** — Part man. Part wolf. 100% crippled. Also including *Punk Rock Nursing Home, Adrift with Space Badgers, Cook for Your Life, Just Another Day in the Park, Frosty and the Full Monty*, and *House of Cats*. **152 pages $10**

BB-132 **"I Knocked Up Satan's Daughter" Carlton Mellick III** — An adorable, violent, fantastical love story. A romantic comedy for the bizarro fiction reader. **152 pages $10**

BB-133 **"A Town Called Suckhole" David W. Barbee** — Far into the future, in the nuclear bowels of post-apocalyptic Dixie, there is a town. A town of derelict mobile homes, ancient junk, and mutant wildlife. A town of slack jawed rednecks who bask in the splendors of moonshine and mud boggin'. A town dedicated to the bloody and demented legacy of the Old South. A town called Suckhole. **144 pages $10**

BB-134 **"Cthulhu Comes to the Vampire Kingdom" Cameron Pierce** — What you'd get if H. P. Lovecraft wrote a Tim Burton animated film. **148 pages $11**

BB-135 **"I am Genghis Cum" Violet LeVoit** — From the savage Arctic tundra to post-partum mutations to your missing daughter's unmarked grave, join visionary madwoman Violet LeVoit in this non-stop eight-story onslaught of full-tilt Bizarro punk lit thrills. **124 pages $9**

BB-136 **"Haunt" Laura Lee Bahr** — A tripping-balls Los Angeles noir, where a mysterious dame drags you through a time-warping Bizarro hall of mirrors. **316 pages $13**

BB-137 **"Amazing Stories of the Flying Spaghetti Monster" edited by Cameron Pierce** — Like an all-spaghetti evening of Adult Swim, the Flying Spaghetti Monster will show you the many realms of His Noodly Appendage. Learn of those who worship him and the lives he touches in distant, mysterious ways. **228 pages $12**

BB-138 **"Wave of Mutilation" Douglas Lain** — A dream-pop exploration of modern architecture and the American identity, *Wave of Mutilation* is a Zen finger trap for the 21st century. **100 pages $8**

BB-139 **"Hooray for Death!" Mykle Hansen** — Famous Author Mykle Hansen draws unconventional humor from deaths tiny and large, and invites you to laugh while you can. **128 pages $10**

BB-140 **"Hypno-hog's Moonshine Monster Jamboree" Andrew Goldfarb** — Hicks, Hogs, Horror! Goldfarb is back with another strange illustrated tale of backwoods weirdness. **120 pages $9**

BB-141 **"Broken Piano For President" Patrick Wensink** — A comic masterpiece about the fast food industry, booze, and the necessity to choose happiness over work and security. **372 pages $15**

BB-142 **"Please Do Not Shoot Me in the Face" Bradley Sands** — A novel in three parts, *Please Do Not Shoot Me in the Face: A Novel*, is the story of one boy detective, the worst ninja in the world, and the great American fast food wars. It is a novel of loss, destruction, and--incredibly--genuine hope. **224 pages $12**

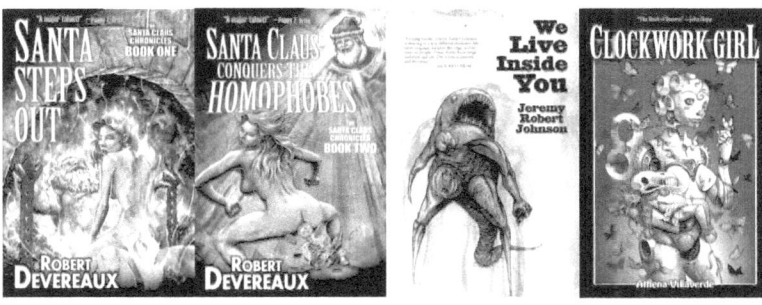

BB-143 **"Santa Steps Out" Robert Devereaux** — Sex, Death, and Santa Claus ... The ultimate erotic Christmas story is back. **294 pages $13**

BB-144 **"Santa Conquers the Homophobes" Robert Devereaux** — "I wish I could hope to ever attain one-thousandth the perversity of Robert Devereaux's toenail clippings." - Poppy Z. Brite **316 pages $13**

BB-145 **"We Live Inside You" Jeremy Robert Johnson** — "Jeremy Robert Johnson is dancing to a way different drummer. He loves language, he loves the edge, and he loves us people. These stories have range and style and wit. This is entertainment... and literature."- Jack Ketchum **188 pages $11**

BB-146 **"Clockwork Girl" Athena Villaverde** — Urban fairy tales for the weird girl in all of us. Like a combination of Francesca Lia Block, Charles de Lint, Kathe Koja, Tim Burton, and Hayao Miyazaki, her stories are cute, kinky, edgy, magical, provocative, and strange, full of poetic imagery and vicious sexuality. **160 pages $10**

BB-147 **"Armadillo Fists" Carlton Mellick III** — A weird-as-hell gangster story set in a world where people drive giant mechanical dinosaurs instead of cars. **168 pages $11**

BB-148 **"Gargoyle Girls of Spider Island" Cameron Pierce** — Four college seniors venture out into open waters for the tropical party weekend of a lifetime. Instead of a teenage sex fantasy, they find themselves in a nightmare of pirates, sharks, and sex-crazed monsters. **100 pages $8**

BB-149 **"The Handsome Squirm" by Carlton Mellick III** — Like Franz Kafka's *The Trial* meets an erotic body horror version of *The Blob*. **158 pages $11**

BB-150 **"Tentacle Death Trip" Jordan Krall** — It's *Death Race 2000* meets H. P. Lovecraft in bizarro author Jordan Krall's best and most suspenseful work to date. **224 pages $12**

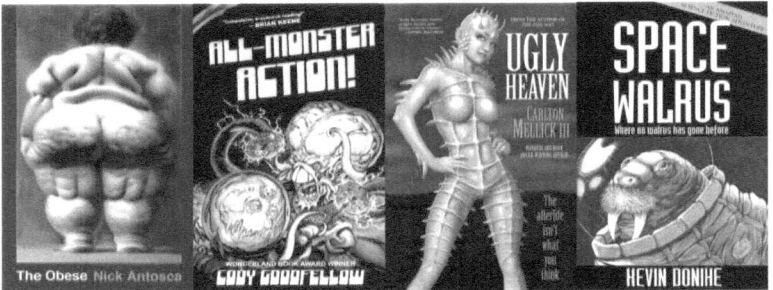

BB-151 **"The Obese" Nick Antosca** — Like Alfred Hitchcock's *The Birds*... but with obese people. **108 pages $10**

BB-152 **"All-Monster Action!" Cody Goodfellow** — The world gave him a blank check and a demand: Create giant monsters to fight our wars. But Dr. Otaku was not satisfied with mere chaos and mass destruction.... **216 pages $12**

BB-153 **"Ugly Heaven" Carlton Mellick III** — Heaven is no longer a paradise. It was once a blissful utopia full of wonders far beyond human comprehension. But the afterlife is now in ruins. It has become an ugly, lonely wasteland populated by strange monstrous beasts, masturbating angels, and sad man-like beings wallowing in the remains of the once-great Kingdom of God. **106 pages $8**

BB-154 **"Space Walrus" Kevin L. Donihe** — Walter is supposed to go where no walrus has ever gone before, but all this astronaut walrus really wants is to take it easy on the intense training, escape the chimpanzee bullies, and win the love of his human trainer Dr. Stephanie. **160 pages $11**

BB-155 **"Unicorn Battle Squad" Kirsten Alene** — Mutant unicorns. A palace with a thousand human legs. The most powerful army on the planet. **192 pages $11**

BB-156 **"Kill Ball" Carlton Mellick III** — In a city where all humans live inside of plastic bubbles, exotic dancers are being murdered in the rubbery streets by a mysterious stalker known only as Kill Ball. **134 pages $10**

BB-157 **"Die You Doughnut Bastards" Cameron Pierce** — The bacon storm is rolling in. We hear the grease and sugar beat against the roof and windows. The doughnut people are attacking. We press close together, forgetting for a moment that we hate each other. **196 pages $11**

BB-158 **"Tumor Fruit" Carlton Mellick III** — Eight desperate castaways find themselves stranded on a mysterious deserted island. They are surrounded by poisonous blue plants and an ocean made of acid. Ravenous creatures lurk in the toxic jungle. The ghostly sound of crying babies can be heard on the wind. **310 pages $13**

BB-159 **"Thunderpussy" David W. Barbee** — When it comes to high-tech global espionage, only one man has the balls to save humanity from the world's most powerful bastards. He's Declan Magpie Bruce, Agent 00X. **136 pages $11**

BB-160 **"Papier Mâché Jesus" Kevin L. Donihe** — Donihe's surreal wit and beautiful mind-bending imagination is on full display with stories such as All Children Go to Hell, Happiness is a Warm Gun, and Swimming in Endless Night. **154 pages $11**

BB-161 **"Cuddly Holocaust" Carlton Mellick III** — The war between humans and toys has come to an end. The toys won. **172 pages $11**

BB-162 **"Hammer Wives" Carlton Mellick III** — Fish-eyed mutants, oceans of insects, and flesh-eating women with hammers for heads. Hammer Wives collects six of his most popular novelettes and short stories. **152 pages $10**